MADALINE GENEVA CLIFTON

Secrets

First published by Madaline Geneva Clifton 2024

Copyright © 2024 by Madaline Geneva Clifton

All rights reserved. No part of this publication may be reproduced, stored or transmitted in any form or by any means, electronic, mechanical, photocopying, recording, scanning, or otherwise without written permission from the publisher. It is illegal to copy this book, post it to a website, or distribute it by any other means without permission.

This novel is entirely a work of fiction. The names, characters and incidents portrayed in it are the work of the author's imagination. Any resemblance to actual persons, living or dead, events or localities is entirely coincidental.

Madaline Geneva Clifton asserts the moral right to be identified as the author of this work.

Madaline Geneva Clifton has no responsibility for the persistence or accuracy of URLs for external or third-party Internet Websites referred to in this publication and does not guarantee that any content on such Websites is, or will remain, accurate or appropriate.

Designations used by companies to distinguish their products are often claimed as trademarks. All brand names and product names used in this book and on its cover are trade names, service marks, trademarks and registered trademarks of their respective owners. The publishers and the book are not associated with any product or vendor mentioned in this book. None of the companies referenced within the book have endorsed the book.

The Book Cover was created using the elements section of Canva Design, filter and effects. In no way is it imperative for the book cover to match the plot, theme or characters of the book even though, for this one, it does. The Book Title does reflect parts of the book. In no way, shape or form is the cover and title misleading or meant to be misleading. I am the sole owner and creator of this work nor does anyone else have my permission to publish my work and they most certainly are not allowed to use it against me.

First edition

This book was professionally typeset on Reedsy.
Find out more at reedsy.com

Contents

Secrets	1
Dedications & Acknowledgements:	3
Chapter One	4
Chapter Two	11
Chapter Three	18
Chapter Four	25
Chapter Five	32
Chapter Six	39
Chapter Seven	46
Chapter Eight	53
Chapter Nine	60
Chapter Ten	67
Chapter Eleven	74
Chapter Twelve	81
Chapter Thirteen	88
Chapter Fourteen	95
Chapter Fifteen	102
Chapter Sixteen	109
Chapter Seventeen	117
Chapter Eighteen	125
About the Author	134

Secrets

"Secrets" is a fantasy novella meant for readers from eighteen plus. It is considered a young adult fiction in my eyes, but there's blood, death and murder mentioned so I couldn't list this short read as such. This is the third, official and original, final edition since I added a new chapter; more or less a bonus chapter that I'm particularly happier with. There's no spice and as far as I've reread there's little to no cussing. This is meant to be a cozy novella as well as a murder mystery.

    I had a few things inspire this book which was meant to be a full length novel, but the story felt finished. It felt like I had come to a conclusion nor did it feel right to drag it out. There are plenty of "secrets" in the small, very much fictional town of Bluebell Springs. Particular places and people also helped to inspire this book—as always, when you blend things; you don't even know who or what did. Also, with that in mind, the main character is partly based on me at the age of eighteen (I didn't party or anything other teens and young adults my age would, didn't feel the need or see the enthusiasm in tragedy); yes, I've had trauma from a young age, but I'd probably still have turned out just as shut off and removed from my peers, because what's the point?

    Everything else in "Secrets" has no correlation to my real

life. It's fictional with loveable and hateable characters that are equally just as fictional. Unlike Sable Darling, I do care about people; she doesn't fully care even when she does. Hope that makes sense. Enough about the novella! Happy reading!

Dedications & Acknowledgements:

"Secrets" is dedicated to those dreaming about escaping reality. To the **READER** who snags a copy in order to purely dive into something new and cozy! I hope this perks up your day in some way. Thank you and thank you for simply existing.

Chapter One

His lips were a carnation pink, soft to the touch with fire in his veins. His cornflower blue eyes danced with a smile as his short, golden, curly hair blew all over the place. He was an eighteen year old fool with a slimness to his body, alabaster skin, broad shoulders, standing at five foot ten. He's a know it all, almost always keeping his nose stuck in a book unless he chose to show off. Girls drool over his appearance, proving just how swoon worthy he is.

My hand chose to press into my cheek as I watched him mingle with Erica Mitchell. I held back a lot of things, barely ceasing to feel any type of way for anyone. My dark pink, full lips became pursed while my candle apple green eyes narrowed on River Treanor. I couldn't believe he was a few months older than me, having grown up next to the blonde. My thick, long, maple brown curls dance as the wind recklessly blows them everywhere striking a pout onto my tan olive features.

I was about five foot two with a petite, slender body as I poked my fork into the food of the school cafeteria. I had heat with River Treanor that he returned tenfold by blatantly ignoring me since the year of me becoming eighteen began. My best friend groaned, pulling me from my thoughts as my sour mood only slightly lifted.

CHAPTER ONE

"Sable, can you believe this?" Roman Treanor is the same age as me with mocha skin, a lean and lankier build, light gray eyes with short, chestnut brown hair. He was about five foot nine while sporting a dark blue leather jacket over a black tee shirt. The wind also ruffled up his hair as his pink lips spiraled down.

I chuckle, lifting an eyebrow, as unemphatic as I had been every single day of my life. I knew people thought of me as strange, weird, odd, and the next upcoming serial killer in the making. They were probably right about that last quip. "What's got you down bad, Lightning Bolt?"

Roman plucked up a tater tot, shoving it viciously into his mouth. He cared too much which was no surprise given he was born on the fourth of July. His face became flushed with pinkness as he violently retrieved something from the pocket of his jacket. "This! This is what's wrong!"

A dark and soft pink letter was shoved onto the top of the picnic table, outside of the school cafeteria. **SLOAN UNIVERSITY, Accepting Submissions for those with special abilities. Submissions close by October 31st, Apply at your own risk.**

My lips were parted in amazement. The light pink glitter reflecting from the letter was enough for me to want to attend and I hate the color pink. **Rolling** my candy apple green eyes, I take a bite from the disgusting sandwich on my plate. "If you mean, this is what's wrong with the world then—"

"No, Sable! That is not what I'm upset about!" Roman hissed, cutting me off as he roughly gripped his hair. He looked on the verge of becoming the next Lex Luthor for how close to bald he was building towards. He took me by shock when he gripped my shoulders which were covered by my dark gray, long sleeve cardigan that acted as a shirt since there were no buttons or zipper.

I tug at my maple brown curls, deeply despising the touching. "Roman, I will bite your hands off!"

A snicker came from the soft pink, full lips of River Treanor as he strode over with his backpack strapped to one shoulder. A half smile clung to those lips as the eighteen year old approached us, catching word of Roman's freakout moment. "Roman, what's your conflict with the ladies? Your freakout will only scare Sable more."

"I'm not scared!" I irritably insist, morbidly disgusted by the touching. Did he not know how to tell the difference between fear and disgust?

His cornflower blue eyes shine with mischief as a smirk graces his lips. He knew what he was doing with his wording. "Are you sure? You seem on edge."

"Well, if you knew anything, especially about girls such as Sable, you would know that she doesn't like touching." Roman scoffs, shaking his head at River. He was side eyeing his brother with a splash of a scowl.

Relief flooded my heart at how well my friend knew me. I see the wheels turning in the dull eyes of the blonde who frowned. I nonchalantly shrug, I shouldn't care about someone who doesn't care about himself. "Roman is pressed about the submissions of Sloan University."

River's cornflower blue eyes widened as he leaned over my shoulder, lifting up the pink letter. He read it over a few times before smirking as if it was a full time job. "Roman, there's no need to be pressed about Sloan University or their submissions. You are such a shoe away from being accepted, that it's not even funny."

Roman scoffed, rolling his light gray eyes. He shook his head, gnawing on his soft pink lips. "I'm not worried about me, you, dunce. Erica."

River chuckles, gesturing to the wheelchair bound girl who was my age and a good friend of mine. "Erica is just getting lunch, she'll be right this way and then you can tell her how much you love her, Roman."

Roman became tense, cutting his light gray eyes to me in order to capture my reaction. "I do not love Erica. You have feelings for her, River."

I fold my arms, becoming quite uncomfortable. I cut my eyes from Roman and River to said girl, rolling up in her wheelchair with her lunch. I wave to Erica who mostly nods as if flabbergasted. "What's with your look of mesmerization?"

"Josh just asked me out. He's so flipping hot." Erica muttered, brushing her golden, silky, long hair into a loose ponytail. Her eyes are a cold blue with her height being about four foot seven with a slim body frame. Her mother didn't particularly enjoy feeding or taking care of her as she should.

I lift my eyebrow at the name, scanning the sea of students until they land on Josh. A scowl pulls my lips into a grimace, aware that he was one of Roman's friends, but a year older than us. "Always older guys, right?"

"Especially the troublemakers." River agreed, cracking a smile as he wanted to tease Erica who he saw as a little sister. His cornflower blue eyes narrowed before cutting to me, making me discomforted just the same.

Roman snorted. "You kid, yes?"

I chuckle at the concern laced in his voice. "Why would I joke about such a thing? Older men are hotter than guys our age. Really, what's the use in having you around?"

Those words cut his heart, allowing the pain to flicker to life in his light gray eyes. His older brother coughed to clear his throat, gathering Roman's attention. "I don't get you, Sable or your logic."

"Older men? You're eighteen. Much like a particular blonde singer, you don't know anything." River informs me, opting to pat the top of my head.

I glare hard-core at him. "Do you know anything, Riv?"

River kept smiling, going so far as to bump his leg into mine.

The interactions caused a smile to bloom on Erica's face. She wasn't one to smile or sport light clothing. She lived her life in darkness including through color which made her even more depressed in her head. "You two are cute. Have you considered dating?"

I burst out laughing at how ridiculous the question was. "Date a loser like River? Good one, Erica. No, he's dating his books which isn't the laughable part."

River furrowed a golden eyebrow, evidently confused as my eyes began to water from my laughter. He cut his eyes to Roman who was tense sitting on my other side. "Laughable? I'm everyone's type!"

Roman scoffed, shaking his head. "If I were a girl and we weren't related; you would not be my type, bro. Don't be so deluded."

"Roman, you wouldn't count either way. You wouldn't be my type in that scenario." River rolled his cornflower blue eyes.

I get my bearings and stop cutting up like it was an impossible task. I wipe away the tears that I produced from my laughing fit. I fold my hands in sync atop of the picnic table. I had grown up in Bluebell Springs which was a rather small town where adventures could be had; if you tried. "You may be hot for someone our age, but you are so nerdy that it's hilarious to

CHAPTER ONE

imagine."

"Don't attempt to not hurt my feelings then proceed to hurt my feelings." River's face was lit red with embarrassment as he bit into his infamous tuna sandwich that he made at home. He preferred them to the school food which was understandable in some cases.

I can fix him, can't I? Or is he just too stuck in his nerdy ways? A cough from Roman stirs on my right with the eighteen year old remaining as unhappy as could be. "What's wrong, Ro?"

Roman narrowed his light gray eyes, setting his jaw into a hard line. He didn't like nicknames. "Sable, what have we spoken about?"

"Your love for sandalwood, the guitar, drums, and Five Seconds of Winter." I tap my fingers on the edge of the concrete picnic table, grinning when Roman blushes. I highly believe it does his skin complexion good, making him less cold in his appearance.

River sighed. "Five Seconds of Winter?"

"An Australian Girl Band. They make pop and rock music." I lightly muse, taking more bites of the gross food on my tray. I'm done with it before the bell for the next class rings.

River is processing the newly received information as something clicks in his brain. He snaps his fingers causing his cornflower blue eyes to widen in realization. "Roman, do you have a crush on them?"

"Why does that have to be the case? I would be lying if I said they were fugly, but they're not. I like their music; take a listen someday—if you need to. Plus, I'm happy to have someone finally representing me and my background." Roman replies, keeping his jaw set with his light gray eyes flickering from his brother to me.

I didn't have to look at either of them to know where they kept staring. Somehow, discomfort covered my skin, making me want to crawl into a hole to hide so they couldn't peer over at me. "Your background?"

"I think he meant his heritage of being mixed. I'm assuming half of this band has half native, half black with one percent of white in their group." River beamed, wiggling his eyebrows at no one in particular.

I don't really care. I process the information, shrugging. "Heritage doesn't matter nor does skin color, as long as they're good with their skills and whatever other talents they have."

Roman sighed. "You don't seem to care about a whole lot, Sable. Why is that?"

Erica had been sitting quietly, eating her lunch, making the best of what little food she did get to eat. She had her entertainment covered. "Unemphatic."

"Exactly. I don't have time to care, Ro. I could care less if River walked out in front of a bus, started singing and the driver ran him down. At the end of the day, nobody would have told him to do such a horrendous act." I mutter, standing up, getting ready to walk off.

Erica, Roman, and River are beyond horrified with my way of words. Their mouths are ajar as I nonchalantly shrug with this gleam in my candy apple green eyes.

Chapter Two

I was at the vending machine, having scored some crunch-tastic Cheetos. I was about to lean on the wall next to the vending machine of snacks when my wrist was grabbed, startling me. A slither of warmth spread through me as a gasp fled my lips. "If you don't let go of me—"

Roman turned me around with a splash of worry in his light gray eyes. He gripped both of my shoulders, doing the one thing I asked of people not to do. His action had my nostrils flaring. "Sable, what is with you? You've never been this unemphatic before."

My eyes are flitting from one mocha hand of his to the other on my shoulders. He was five foot nine which meant he was about seven inches taller. I was about to break his wrists if he kept his hands on me as sadness swept into my brain. "Move your hands!"

"Why? What have you got against touching?" Roman's light gray eyes tried to scan my candy apple green ones. He frowned at noting how I wouldn't look his way when he was invading my personal space. He huffed, dropping his hands from my shoulders.

My formerly enthused eyes were void of emotion as they heatedly glared up at him. "I have always been as unemphatic as you presume I haven't been. When have you ever seen me care or cry?"

"Sable—" Roman searched his brain for words to say when I plucked open my bag of Cheetos. He was at a loss for words when I lifted a dust covered finger to his lips. He lifted an eyebrow at the orange Cheetos dust as if I were insane. "How could you not have sympathy for anyone else?"

I take a beat to process his question before nonchalantly shrugging. In a sort of way, I guess I'm unhinged. I drop my finger from his lips before leaning on the wall next to the vending machine. Relief floods the hunger in my stomach as I crunch on the Cheetos; lunch just didn't do it for me. "I have unspoken issues. Take it up with Maria."

"Maria." Roman muttered, rolling his light gray eyes as he came to mirror my action. He managed to lightly graze me as the bitterness of the middle Treanor brother sparked to life. It was his daily routine. "Maria Darling, a twenty nine year old, married your dad, two years ago. Did she get caught up in a car crash?"

I snort at the question. I think he's lost it. "Why would that even be a question you would ask? She's a business manager, unknownst to me. I'm fairly certain she will not be crashing her pink Mercedes."

Roman chuckled, nudging my shoulder with his. He had a face for a smile and a major love for the girls. "I had to ask. What issues do you have aside from the fact that you need an attitude adjustment?"

Those words from his mouth did more than sting me. They bothered me to the point of a fantasy about snapping his neck popped into my mind. I shake it off with a secret desire of blood thirst lurking around the corner. I pop another Cheeto into my mouth, cutting my eyes to a few students wandering in whichever direction.

"An attitude adjustment? Don't lecture me, Ro. You blow up at your poor mom for every single thing all because of your father. He was the problem, not her." I irritably reiterate to the brunette who pouts, plucking the bag of Cheetos from my hand. I groan, trying to snatch them back but he hides them from view.

There's this nasty gleam that has taken over his beautiful, light gray eyes. He isn't himself as he keeps me from the one thing that would sooth the savage beast within. "Do you really want to play that with me, Sable Adele Darling?"

"Roman—" I open my mouth to protest, hating that nasty gleam in his eyes. I hadn't seen him turn that nasty on me since we were ten years old. I found a friend of River's quite charming—being blonde and all only to share a kiss with said blonde boy. To me, it meant nothing, but it somehow angered Roman and shocked River. I sighed.

"Sable, do you not remember what you did to me when we were ten years old?" Roman asks as if being a mindless kid of not understanding made a lick of sense to bring up. His eyes were blazing with rage causing me to purse my lips. He looked darker than the blood thirst I had been prone to moments prior. He was more of a wild, sarcastic, hot head who didn't care about who he hurt.

I fold my arms to my bosom. "I did nothing to you at ten years old. I was a kid. Can you give me back my Cheetos?"

Roman analyzed my eyes and my body purposely dropping my bag of Cheetos in the trashcan. He maliciously smiled as if his action would put me off of food. "If you want to dig for them then sure."

I walk over to the trashcan with this stoic look on my face. I drop my backpack by the can on the concrete ground before plucking my Cheetos from the trash. I proceed to plop some more of them directly into my mouth, smirking as he winces. "Ro, I do not know what your deal is, but testing me is not a good idea."

Roman watched my every move as the nastiness within seemed to be fading from view. Sadness swept into his light gray eyes once I twirled around to face him again. "Sable, I'm sorry."

Rolling my candy apple green eyes. My sour mood doesn't once lift. Why would I become energetic from his apology? I don't care that he seems upset because of his actions on my behalf. "It's funny how you think I care. I just don't."

"You are a teenage girl. You're going to be moody and shut off. I shouldn't think anything is truly wrong with you." Roman replied as he hung his head in defeat. He could have been on the cusp of telling me that he loves me and I'd have to walk away, shrugging with no care in the world.

Boys and men were all about themselves—what they could get. They craved holding the opposite sex back, to ruin our chances of knowing we don't need them.

Light gray eyes peer up at me through thick, long, black lashes. His eyes connect with mine, nearly on a deeper level.

I frown. "Did I speak my thoughts aloud?"

Pressing a finger to his temple, he shook his head. His eyes were trained on me as if my thoughts were infiltrating his. He didn't look happy nor could I blame him.

No, really, I can't fix him or anyone. I can't even fix myself.

"Is that how you truly see boys and men?" Roman inquired, pulling away from my mind.

CHAPTER TWO

I finished my Cheetos with a quickness, fidgeting where I was standing. Biting my lower lip in a pout due to the agitation brewing—mostly between us. I process the fact that he was in my head, despising him more. "Thank you, Captain Obvious. That is exactly how I see boys and men. You briefly got nasty with me because you're stuck in the playground. Girls mature quicker, faster—that's why we prefer older guys."

The sting in his gray eyes was surreal. Roman licked the side of his mouth. "I…I don't think you should keep speaking. Older guys are just the same, just adult men who would rather take advantage of you in our place."

"Is River like that?" I inquired as a smirk dashed across my face. I saw his mood sink further below the waves that were crashing with temperament. I am fond of blonde guys, always have been. I had yet to feel the warm, fuzzy, tingly emotion everyone in love or falling in love got slammed with.

"You are not asking about River. Not in this life, not in any lives." Roman spoke with venom in his voice, a storm in his eyes, and heartbreak in his body.

"How about I ask River myself? I'm sure he would be more than happy to answer my question. You're too bent to be of any use to anyone but yourself." I remark to Roman who is astonished at how cold I could be.

"You will not ask him anything of that nature." Roman had this plea in his voice, inching closer to me.

My posture straightened as alarm shot through every fiber of my body. My eyes dart from head to toe of Roman, extending my hands so he doesn't cross the boundary of my personal space. "If you attempt to touch me again, I will snap the bones in both of your hands. Good luck playing the guitar and drums afterwards."

The snarl in my voice didn't go missed by Roman. He kept a distance from me with the urge to comfort me by a hug. He was quite obvious with his intentions lacing confusion in my head. "You're my best friend, Sable. What's with the judgment, all of a sudden?"

"I'm not trying to judge you, Ro. You are putting pressure on me—pressure I don't want. We're both eighteen years old with plenty of life left to live. Don't settle for less than." I softly muse with no affection in my voice. My voice is strained, yearning for a separation from him.

Roman wasn't somebody I had ever once thought I should be parted from. His actions and words this fall evening, at school, proved different. He needs to move on with his life and find someone who would give him affection. "Sable—"

Another plea in his tone as if his whining was going to change my mind. *Lightning in a bottle.* Inhaling sharply, I opt to rip off the bandaid. "Ro, don't make this more difficult for either of us. You were my best friend up until your heartbreaking confession. If I'm attracted to any kind of guy; it's blonde guys. Sorry."

Roman deflated as quick as the warm light of day we had, sitting at the picnic table outside. His bottom lip began to quiver, stirring some guilt trapped within the bottom of my soul. He took a few deep breaths. "I should be used to rejection."

"Oh, who has rejected you? All the girls love you." I make sure to correct my best friend. I know I said he wasn't my best friend, but I just needed space to collect myself. I also believe he needs space to do the same.

"I don't care about any of them. Whatsoever." Roman hissed as silent as could be. He wasn't so much angry as he was hurt. He craved something, someone he couldn't have, not meant for him.

"Erica?" I sheepishly ask, rubbing the back of my neck. I watch Roman scowl, before the boy folds his arms to his blue leather clad chest with the black tee shirt he favored.

Roman briefly presses fingers to his forehead before shaking his head. "There's only one girl I care about and will only ever have cared about. She's evidently insane, reckless and cold."

"Oof." I snort before adding an afterthought. "She sounds like a mirror reflection of…well, you."

Roman was horrified. "Sable, I was talking about—"

I hold up my hand to cut him off. I walk off in the direction I need to go in order to finish out the school day. I was not about to hear my best friend out. I couldn't.

Chapter Three

"Sable?" The hiss of River's annoying voice came just as I rushed from my final class of the day. How was he so close when we weren't even in the same year?

To be rude or not to be? I ponder the question, tensing when his hand clamps down on my shoulder. I glare daggers at said hand until the blonde realizes his mistake, profusely apologizing. "River? I have to go home. Why are you bothering me?"

"Sable, I'm not trying to bother you. River told me you aren't friends anymore. I wanted to ensure that you were okay." River sheepishly spoke, toying with the gnape of his neck. He seemed nervous.

"I'm alright." My tone is strained upon answering the blonde who still had his hand on my shoulder. I lightly tap his hand. "Shouldn't you be moving this thing or do you prefer for it to be surgically removed via my teeth?"

"I got your crazy." River said, removing his hand from my shoulder. He stuck his hands into the depths of his blue jeans as the navy green knit sweater on his body wrinkled with movement. He wasn't done with bothering me. "Sable, you two have been best friends since you were toddlers."

I rolled my candy apple green eyes at how little truth there was in those words. "Riv, Roman and I briefly stopped being best friends for a period in our childhood. It was over some silly-like crush on one of your friends. Didn't sit well with him."

"I think I remember that incident. Didn't think it was that big of a deal." River said, solemn as he shrugged it off. His cornflower blue eyes danced as he stuck by me, gently brushing his shoulder against mine.

"I have always felt some type of way for blonde guys. It wasn't a big deal to me, still isn't, but apparently, your brother holds a grudge." I reply as dry as can be.

River becomes thoughtful with the detailed piece of information. He lifted up a hand as he spoke his younger brother's name into existence. "Did you forget about Theodore?"

"He's a fifteen year old, wannabe writer who enjoys black and yellow plaid, flannel, all that crazed with a black trenchcoat. He's not special. Of course, I remember Theo. I see the annoying little boy everyday." I vent as River chuckles.

"What a deep way to describe either of my brother's." River laughed when the words left his soft pink lips. He was sweet and cute, but he was competitive with a streak of annoyance and low tolerance for those around him. It didn't matter how important any of us were to him; when his temper flared—duck and cover.

"Um, if you want me to describe Roman then that would not be how I would describe him." I sighed, correcting the fact that River tried to make it seem either or for the younger Treanor boys.

"SABLE ADELE DARLING!" The shrill voice of Tara Jessup infiltrated the school atmosphere, seeing students evaporate in smoke just to avoid the Queen of Evil. She's got a brown complexion with dark eyes, standing at five foot four with a thin waistline. She's unusually beautiful, popular and easy to influence people.

River gestured for me to enter into a vacant classroom as my heart picked up speed, racing like no tomorrow. He knew the snide remarks I had made to piss her off even after I apologized. He talked sense into me when I once upon a time believed I knew better. "She won't find you, in here, with me. We can nerd out together."

I was legitimately shoved by River Treanor into a vacant classroom, groaning as I was slammed into a desk chair and table attached. I shot the blonde boy a glare of daggers as soon as I twirled about face. "Hey, Riv?"

"Yes, Sae?" River inquires, giving me a nickname. He briefly cut his eyes to me when I voiced my curious question.

"Would it be alright if I slam you into the desk like a maniac with no respect, manners, or like you were raised like a misbehaved pig?" I inquire, giving River an earful. I see his pale features turn into a blush, but was it due to embarrassment?

The cream colored door of the classroom flew open, knocking River right into me. He groaned, profusely apologizing to me as his cornflower blue eyes met my candy apple green ones in utter shock. He was horrified. "Sae, I didn't...I'm sorry."

I lost the oxygen from my lungs when the impact of a heavier body hit me. A scowl slithered into my eyes when I looked up to see Tara, snickering in the doorway. "What do you want, Tara Jessup?"

"I want your head on a platter, Sable Darling. You victimized me by saying hurtful things to me." Tara whimpered, keeping a hand lifted in the air. She had long transferred to Sloan University which everyone in Bluebell Springs knew about.

My eyes glossed over with lazy, careless, unconcern. "I did

apologize to you, Tara. It turned out that you were dearly disturbed and I shouldn't have said or acted indifferent."

"Indifferent." River whispered, averting his cornflower blue eyes to the checkered floor of the Bluebell Springs High School. His mind is connecting the dots that previously hadn't been connected.

Tara grinds her teeth, working her jaw as she balls up her fist. She didn't care that I had apologized, she just cared that my image was ruined. "I don't care about your apology or the fact that I'm playing the victim; feigning as if I have a mental illness, Sable. I care about ruining your reputation, burning it to the ground."

Parting his soft pink lips, River cut his eyes from Tara to me. He wasn't sure how to form his next sentence. "Why would you openly admit to us that your mental illness is fake and that you just care about ruining somebody else's reputation? Where's the logic?"

Tara was aggravated—perturbed even. She shook her head with dark eyes becoming flabbergasted. "I don't know why I would admit such a thing. I don't know how I could speak my mind without filtering it."

I tilt my head sideways as something clicks in my brain. I had a knack for a no filter zone. What if I had some type of special ability? Would that make me more of a freak to my peers? Sure, but who truly gave a flying truck? Pressing my dark pink lips together, having yet to shove River from being so close to me, I clear my throat.

"So, Tara, what's really with your vendetta against me?" I inquire, giving her a listening ear as a smidge of barely noticeable, light pink glitter falls from my hand.

Tara inhales sharply, slowly exhaling as the eighteen year old in red and gray comes clean. She couldn't bite her tongue this time. "My dad is the biggest slut in the universe! It doesn't help that my mom is the exact mirror image of him! I just want my parents to love each other and to love me."

Tears surfaced in her dark eyes as amazement came to life within me. I seemed to be able to get her to speak the truth and lay a confession of sins on us. I had long winced at her use of the word, slut. "Have you talked to your parents about their behavior?"

"I've tried numerous times. They don't want to hear me out." Tara said as the hate in her heart evaporated when her troubles came rushing from her lips. She folded her arms over the vibrant, cherry, red, blazer clinging to her arms while tapping her fingers as if slightly impatient.

"You may have to force them to listen to you." I gently replied, being as delicate with Tara as I could.

River brushed against me by mistake causing his face to redden at the accident. He opened his mouth to profusely apologize. "I didn't mean to—"

"Riv, shush." I dryly responded with my eyes trained on Tara, doing what I could to come up with a plan. How could you make your parents listen to you if they didn't want to listen to you? "Sit them down, even if you have to talk to them separately and make them hear you out. They should be willing to listen to their children."

River pinched the bridge of his nose, agreeing in silence before he spoke his mind. "Parents should be willing to listen to their children, but they don't always so it ends up in divorce. My father was busy wanting to do his own thing, too busy to care about my mother or me…"

Pressing a finger to his lips to shush him, I vigorously shook my head at River. I couldn't let the blonde make the current situation about himself. "River, this isn't about you and your formerly broken family. Okay?"

River closed his mouth, nodding along as he clamped his mouth down shut. His eyes held empathy for Tara. "Tara, is there anything we can do to help? Instead of bullying, why not ask for our help or advice?"

"I seriously hadn't thought about that." Tara said with sadness appearing in her dark eyes, making me believe she was depressed.

Guilt tugged on my heartstrings causing me to cough to clear my throat. I didn't have much more to offer Tara. "I don't have much else to offer you in advice. Just try to get them to listen in any way, shape or form that you can."

"Okay." Tara said, nodding as more pink glitter slipped from my hand; this time in a dark pink glow that formed a cloud around her head.

"What do you think is with that dark pink cloud intermingled with the light pink glitter?" I mutter to River once Tara nods, strutting off—soon to forget the conversation we ever had.

River straightened his posture, leaning into me on the desk. He had still been pressed low into me from where Tara had used the door to slam him into me. He didn't want to risk anymore anger from the mean girl, sighing when she was gone. "I don't know, but isn't it obvious?"

I fight a smirk, enjoying the calm side of the blonde boy. "Isn't what, obvious?"

"You have special abilities." River softly mumbles, wiggling his eyebrows at me. His words struck a nerve wracking chord in me.

"What type of special abilities though, River?" I gently muse in turn, aware that I could attend Sloan University if I ever chose to apply. I nonchalantly shrug, knowing I wouldn't. "If you are thinking about me attending Sloan University—don't. People already label me as a freak."

River raised a dark blonde eyebrow, making a special point to brush against me as something stirs within. "I think you have the ability to make people confess nerve wracking truths. A type of manipulation in dark pink with a sprinkle of light glitter."

"Interesting theory, Rivvie." I voice, tapping my fingers on my arms after folding them to my bosom. I push myself from leaning on the desk in order to exit the classroom. I should have been heading home since the school day was over.

River scoffed, chuckling as he caught up to me. "It isn't a theory, Sae. I saw you work some special mojo."

My laughter becomes nervous as I place my hand over my chest. How could my emotions start buzzing suddenly? Was I a late bloomer compared to the rest of my peers? I yearned to care more about the things I should as an eighteen year old, but I just didn't. On my walk home, I will be playing my music, ignoring the noise from those around me.

Chapter Four

My headphones were glued to my ears upon entering the cream, one story, brown tiled roof of 513 Pied Piper Avenue. I was listening to my favorite artist, re-energizing my mood as I swept into the house. I was thankful for my gray knit cardigan and black snug fitting jeans with black hiking boots. A shiver had passed me by as the wind roared on my walk home. I was bobbing my head to a great jam when my gray and black headphones were ripped from my head.

"SABLE ADELE DARLING? WHERE HAVE YOU BEEN?!" The shrill, honey-like voice of my stepmother roared in agony. Her gray eyes widen in emphasis with each layered word. Her lengthy, wavy, jet black hair was pinned. Maria Darling has model features with a slender body, gold skin, standing at five foot four. She was twenty nine years of age, definitely too young to be a step-mother.

"School." I scowl as I attempt to snatch back my headphones. I watch the woman put her ear up to my headphones, making this disgusted face.

"Please tell me that is not who I think it is." Maria gags, shaking her head. She's in her gray blazer over a black button up long sleeve, tucked into a lengthy gray pencil skirt with gray high heels to match. Her lips were painted a vibrant red color.

"It's exactly who you think it is. I love him and promise to grow up and marry him." I grin, watching the horror become even more transparent on her face.

"Don't be sick, Sable. He's a fifty year old, white rapper with no talent and a deep hatred for women except his own daughters." Maria irritably ranted as I snatched my headphones back.

"Well, sorry about your luck, Maria, but that's my future husband you're trashing." I continue pulling her leg, watching the horror within my step-mother grow. I tap my fingers to my chin. "Didn't you marry a fifty year old man with no morals and a hard-on for young women?"

"Yes, but…this isn't about me!" Maria hissed, shaking her head. She was able to fight against whatever manipulation River insisted I had. She walked over to the counter of our house in the kitchen, knocking on a dark pink flier. "Pack your bags, Sable. This is your last night in this house!"

"Whoa! Whoa! You can't kick me out!" I sharply hissed as my good mood of picking on my step-mother became sour. I didn't mean to upset her so much that she decided to be done with me. Is it even legal in Bluebell Springs to toss your kin out on the streets even if they are barely of age?

"No, Sable. I'm not kicking you out of your own house. That's an illegal act in Bluebell Springs even if you are considered a legal adult. I am taking you to Sloan University, you were accepted into their school. I sent a submission for you and Lila a while ago." Maria softly muttered, actually having been thoughtful.

My step-mother wasn't the devil incarnate or bad boned let alone ill intentioned. There were things she did that I just didn't agree with; marrying an old geezer was one of those things.

CHAPTER FOUR

"Where is Lila?"

"Your sister is already at Sloan University." Maria simply remarked, half smiling.

Lila Darling is twenty with tan skin, a semi curvy figure, standing at five foot eleven with hazel green eyes and long, wavy, auburn hair. The twenty year old with a fascination for purple had freckles galore, making one question everything. She was a smart cookie with a love for books, true crime and the medical field. How could my older sister have gotten caught up in a school such as Sloan University?

"She was accepted into a school full of freaks?" I inquire as Maria walks around me, scurrying off towards my bedroom. I'm too stunned to move or realize what's happening. I open my mouth only to close my mouth, not wanting to attend Sloan University; thinking back on the disgust within Roman when he brought it up.

"I got your stuff. I already had a bag packed for you, just in case." Maria grinned, ushering me from the house I had grown up in. She was able to move me from inside the house while numbness washed over me.

How could someone do something without my input? I shake my head at Maria as soon as my brain catches up to the numb of my body and the shock in my head. "Why are you so eager to drop me off at some random school with random people?"

Smiling at me, Maria shrugs, not believing it to be a big deal. She was able to get me into her pink Mercedes, zooming up to the front gate of the black fence of the school. "This is your new home, Sable. I'm sorry it had to come to this, but it is what it is."

I heard the shallowness of her tone causing my maple brown eyebrows to draw together. What is up with her? How could my father want this for me or my sister unless something happened? I refuse to exit her vehicle, barely eyeing the lengthy, smooth, pink building of Sloan University with a water fountain and a garden at the front, close to the entrance of the school. "My father would not send us away."

"Sable, you are so right. Your father would not want this life for you, but your father is gone—forevermore. You'll just have to accept it as I'm having to." Maria said, reaching over me to open the passenger side of the door. She was so quick to get me to the school with me unaware of what was zooming past us.

"I don't want this." I inform Maria who shrugs, nudging me from her pink vehicle.

"I didn't want children, Sable. What's your point?" Maria irritably scoffs, viciously plucking up the pink suitcase with my stuff in it. She violently flings it to me which I sidestep so it doesn't bring my body harm.

I step up to the passenger side of the door which she is quick to slam shut. My candy apple green eyes brighten with a hint of worry. "Ria, what the actual—?"

"Sorry about your luck, Sable." Maria softly muttered before driving off as quickly as she had driven me to the loony bin.

My heart shattered, knowing that the Treanor brothers wouldn't look at me the same way ever again. I was about to give up all hope when the clearing of a throat belonging to an unfamiliar person came from beside me. "Hey!"

"I am Taylor Marsh. I will be your guide." A six foot one, nineteen year old with porcelain skin, freckles, aquamarine green eyes, and curly, short, fiery, strawberry blonde hair spoke. He was lean, lanky, reminding me of a bit of a nerd in a soft blue hoodie with gray sweatpants.

CHAPTER FOUR

"No." I irritably bite off as he nervously chuckles.

"You have no choice. You're stuck with us, Sable Darling. Either you can choose to walk into Sloan University or I can carry you." Taylor half joked, mostly serious as something cold clung to his green eyes.

I roll my candy apple green eyes, nonchalantly shrugging. "Good luck. I—"

Taylor plastered a fake smile onto his face, keeping to his promise. He picked me up, slung me over one shoulder then proceeded to grab my suitcase with his free hand. He was able to cause me second hand embarrassment nor did it seem to be a very real factor within me to become embarrassed especially given my lack of empathy for everyday humans. "You'll find you will either listen or own up to the consequences of your bad decisions."

My face is pink as he sets me to my feet upon shutting the stone, white door once we're in the school. My green eyes scan the maroon carpet with marble white walls coating the inside of the place. I shouldn't be embarrassed especially since none of the strangers at Sloan University were familiar to me. "That's not as embarrassing as you think it is."

"Welcome to Sloan University! We look to hone your special abilities and help you craft them beautifully. Unless you turn out to be a serial killer then we hope to remove your powers and take your soul." Taylor said with a tinge of unease in his voice while walking towards stairs that rotated back and forth in the same spot.

"I can't…wait, Strawberry, slow down. My brain is about as slow as can be." My cheeks remain flushed as I hurry to keep up with him.

Taylor stopped at the foot of the gray, marble stairs. His

strawberry blonde eyebrows met his hairline, thinking me ludicrous. His aquamarine eyes said as much, leading doubt into my heart. "Sable, you may believe you're slow, but you aren't."

"Taylor Marsh? Do you perhaps know Erica and Gavin Mitchell?" I ask once my brain finishes wrapping around everything that had taken place once I got home from Bluebell Springs High.

"No." Taylor says, pursing his soft pink lips before shaking his head. "You seem to be able to 'manipulate' as detailed by your step-mother on your application form."

"She's the hoe with daddy issues." I irritably voice, gaining an uneasy smile from Taylor.

Taylor gestures to the stairs. "We are headed to your dormitory."

I nod my head, following after the redhead in complete silence. I hadn't caught sight of my big sister yet. I'm led to a dorm with my name in a silver plaque written across it. "Shouldn't there be more than one person in a dorm?"

Taylor chuckles, shaking his head at the notion. "Are you insane, Sable Darling? We all have our own dormitory-like apartments. Nobody knows how long we'll have to hone our abilities. We could be well into our thirties when we are able to take control of our abilities."

I process his words, shaking my head at him. I'm beyond annoyed by the idea of being away from home especially when Lila hadn't appeared, as of yet. I had to wonder if my sister was somehow being brainwashed. "I cannot afford to be here in my thirties."

"You're adorable, Sable." Taylor softly mumbled, lightly tapping my nose. He cleared his throat as something clicked in his mind. "Those attending Sloan University are required to wear a certain color with a particular dress code. Red, black, and pink are our standard slash traditional colors."

I lifted an eyebrow, sensing there was more to the story. I was also waiting for Taylor to open the door to my dorm, making the mental note that the door was a powder blue. "I sense there's more to your story."

"Special, high ranking students get different color treatments. You will be required to wear powder blue and gray, making you off limits for several reasons." Taylor harshly gulped, before tugging at the collar of his hoodie.

"You're wearing a soft blue. I'm going to assume you're special." I gently replied, half smirking as Taylor grew deeply uncomfortable.

Taylor nonchalantly shrugged. "Some of us are almost like teacher's pets to the headmaster. I don't mean that in a bad or perverted way. He's not a monster, but he's got a way with making particular students feel special."

I snort, unsure I believed Taylor. If the headmaster of Sloan University made them feel special; he had to be a monster. I'm fairly certain there's no way around it. I laugh out loud. "Your headmaster is definitely a monster. If he makes the students here feel special—"

"Once you meet the headmaster, you won't be speaking so ill of a decent man. He's not what you're painting him to be in your head. In the future, I will word my sentences better so they aren't taken out of context." Taylor swiftly informed me, kicking himself into the ground. He had betrayed himself and his beloved headmaster.

Chapter Five

I rapidly blinked upon Taylor opening the dorm with my name on it when powder blue walls and dark blue carpet breach my line of vision. I could not believe my terrible luck as tears shrouded my eyesight. I rub the tears away, attempting to let my sensitive eyes adjust to the beautiful, calming color. "This is too much."

"You'll adjust. We all do." Taylor gently mused, gently squeezing my shoulder. His action caused me to clench my jaw, on the cusp of grinding my teeth. He furrowed his eyebrows when he realized he had irritated me beyond recognition. He slowly removed his hand from my shoulder; stirring a sense of relief in my heart.

"DO NOT ever touch me again." I bitterly remark to the redhead. I cut my eyes to the uniform laying on the foot of my bed on a black wooden trunk. Rolling my candy apple green eyes, I cannot believe it. "A black mini skirt? Black sweatpants I could understand, but who wants some weirdo staring up their skirts?"

"You could voice your concerns to Headmaster Jones." Taylor mused, causing me to weave my eyebrows in unison. He hummed as something struck him as odd, opting to voice them as he ushered me from the dorm. "Black mini skirt and

CHAPTER FIVE

sweatpants? They told me gray. Must have been wrong."

I lift a hand to stop the nineteen year old from waving me from the dorm. I leave my pink, fugly suitcase at the bottom of the bed. "Headmaster Jones?"

"His last name is Jones. He uses his first name in some cases. Like I said, some students are more special in his eyes than others." Taylor nonchalantly shrugs, gaining a sigh of annoyance from me.

I grit my teeth, wondering if Maria was even being honest about dropping me off. Or did the lunatic convince my father to abandon me? I quirk an eyebrow when Taylor tosses a powder blue blazer at my face. "Why are you trying to smother me with this thing?"

"Put it on. I have to show you the school then take you to meet Headmaster Jones." Taylor urges with a smile glued to his face. His eyes held a falsetto causing me to silently groan.

I want to know where all the nice, normal people are— already, missing my friends. I missed River, Roman and Erica. I pinch the bridge of my forehead. "I am not visiting with your Headmaster. I just got here."

"You are. Do you want me to drag you to his office?" Taylor inquired, allowing his barely visible eyebrows to connect with his hairline. His words had me rethinking every choice I ever made.

"I'll show you what I'm made of, if you dare consider that a viable option." I hissed in response to Taylor. I toss the powder blue blazer onto the bed, made of black oak; made up of a powder blue duvet with white bed linen. I speak before he can speak up. "Before you threaten me, I am at least not wearing that. I have had enough school for one single day."

"I love that you think, showing up means sitting on those

abilities you have. We don't do that here. You are one of those who have night classes." Taylor softly muses with a twinkle in his eyes. His eyes matched my own in not caring as if equally as unemphatic.

I start chewing the inside of my cheek. "Taylor, I'm not—"

Taylor lifted a finger to interrupt me. He chose to bend around me, picking up the blazer. He held it in front of me. "Until you put on your blazer, we can have a stare off. You won't win."

I try not to grind my teeth. I keep my mouth pressed into a hard line, taking him up on the offer. "Fine. Have it your way."

Taylor seemed deeply disturbed by my lack of motivation to do what he wanted me to do. If he and I had anything in common then we'd be on the next level of insanity. "The faster you put this blazer on—"

I side step the redhead, heading for the exit of the dorm. I step into the hall of dark blue carpet on the second floor with maroon walls. In the dorm section, that's how you could tell you were headed for your bed or so I'll take the wild guess. I walk to the railing of the second floor, eyeing the students on the first floor; coming and going. "Are you coming, Taylor?"

Rolling his aquamarine green eyes, Taylor clings to the powder blue blazer; stuffing it into my arms. "Put it on!"

"No." I hiss in reply to Taylor while narrowing my eyes, searching the rejection in his gaze. How many times did people have to tell him off in order for him to get the hint? I scoff as I purposely drop the powder blue blazer to the floor of Sloan University, yearning for my normalcy to return. "I will not be attending night classes."

"It's a part of your requirement to attend Sloan University. You can't go back to Bluebell Springs High." Taylor urgently mutters.

A man from my right leans on the rails as casually as possible. He's fit with broad shoulders, tanned skin, standing at five foot nine with a neatly, trimmed black beard. He seems nonchalant, gathering our attention when he clears his throat as if he had something urgent to say. He was wearing a white baseball cap in order to hide his short, black hair, matching his beard. "Ladies, are you two done arguing?"

Taylor Marsh began to profusely sweat, becoming clammy. "Sir, I—"

The man held up a hand to stop Taylor mid-sentence. "Let the lady speak. You won't be attending night classes, why?"

I was more than reluctant to unfold my arms but did so anyway, becoming sheepish and shy; all of a sudden. I eye the man, not sure what business it was of his. "Night classes are for the weak and some of us need to sleep. Sorry."

"Did your folks not discuss your attendance at Sloan University or did they leave you with little to no explanation?" The Headmaster inquired, allowing his eyes to roam from head to toe of my body.

"From just a guess, you must be Headmaster Jones." I remark, inching closer from the man, towards Taylor. His vibes were darker than Jackie Chan. "They didn't, but I already don't like you."

"Yes, I am Headmaster Jones. Amir Jones. Guess what, Sable? You don't have to like me to attend Sloan University?" Amir spoke, extending a hand towards me. He was a bit rough around the edges with blue eyes peeking from underneath his hat.

"I will not be shaking hands with you." I inform the thirty something year old man, wiping a free hand down the leg of my black jeans. I wasn't just put off by the man; a growing, concerning attraction began in the pit of my stomach towards the thirty year old male. A scowl slides onto my face as something clicks in his brain.

"You need to take it up with your father. Maria evidently did not explain anything to you before she rudely dropped you off on our doorstep. I apologize." Amir voices, ogling the students from over the railing. He's making sure they get to their respective classes without slacking off.

"And, you can't explain whatever it is, to me?" I challenge, quirking an eyebrow as the man strokes his beard before pulling away from the railing.

"It would be a very simple, easy, explanation. It really would be, but is it my place?" Amir said, briefly pressing a hand over his heart. His eyes were darting everywhere, not keeping a steady hold until he sighed. He didn't think his annoyance for the day could pique. He motioned for me to follow him, causing me to roll my eyes.

A shove of my shoulder came from Taylor who leveled his own set of green eyes to make sure I understood him correctly. I finally took the powder blue blazer which he had so lovingly plucked from the floor while I wasn't looking. I take deep breaths as my nerves fidget to life causing me to toy with my fingers.

"Thank you for not talking back." Taylor whispered, causing his breath to fan my ear.

I grow uncomfortable, shaking my head, ready to tell him off. I focus on the journey to the office of Headmaster Jones. A shudder stems from me upon just thinking of the name. *Headmaster?* I would rather not be using the term since I wasn't in a fictional book of fictional worlds. "I save all my backtalk for the ones creating warmth in my heart."

CHAPTER FIVE

"What warmth?" Taylor asked, lifting an eyebrow as my face fell.

I don't utter another word to him as I walk into the office of Amir Jones. I find it weird how he walks over to his pool table, gesturing for us to join him. "So, what exactly did they not explain to me? Maria pretty much just dropped me off, mentioning how I wasn't her problem anymore or something along those twisted lines."

"Nothing is wrong with Nicholas Darling. Your father should have been the one to drive you over, explaining the rules and such." Amir says, cleaning a cue stick to play one on one pool with himself. He uses the stick to poke a set of cue balls on said table, gaining an eye roll from me.

"Maria explained nothing while driving me over." I reiterate, causing the man to nod.

Amir isn't leaning on the pool table anymore as he sets the stick down on said table. He leans on it, eyeing us; mostly me. "Your father wanted you to attend Sloan University aware of the manipulation ability you have; along with a more worrying aspect of your ability. It's definitely not my place."

"How about I reach her father for you?" Taylor adds his two cents, gaining a nod from Amir who strokes his beard some more.

What was with idiot men stroking their beards while more pressing matters took place? I snap my fingers to regain his attention, noting pink dust rubbing from off of my fingers via the action. "How is it not your place to tell me? I'm eighteen, inching closer to nineteen every single day."

His lips twitched at the mention before a coy smile almost brokered his face. "Exactly, Miss Sable. You are of age which means I should be able to tell you but, it is far from my place to speak to you about the truth, your origins and the concerning matter at hand. It is within your father's job to explain to you as much."

"So, does this mean I won't be forced to attend classes at night here?" I ask with relief building in the pit of my stomach.

"How about evening classes and you don't have to live here?" Amir mumbles, relieved when an eager Taylor returns; accompanied by the likes of a disheveled Nicholas Darling.

"Nicholas, I'll say this once; you best hear me—if your wife drops off another of your children with no warning to live full time…" Amir trailed off, cutting his blue eyes to me before coming up short. He shook his head, removing the white baseball cap from his short, black hair. He was definitely handsome; a bit bitter and over the top a jerk.

Nicholas began to sweat, casting his candy apple green eyes towards me. "I had no idea Maria drove Sable away. I'll have a stern talk with her. She usually doesn't act out that much."

I refrain from allowing Nicholas Darling to hug me.

His legs are a bit weird looking with short, dirty blonde hair. He's got a nice tan, thin and crusted pink lips. He was about six foot two with broad shoulders; **decent** looking for a man of his age.

"Dad, I don't hug and we all know this." I sharply hissed at the man, clinging to the powder blue blazer before exiting the powder blue and brown office. I don't care if my father is following along as I breeze towards the front doors of Sloan University. I am not sticking around.

Chapter Six

"Dad, what is going on?" I ask once we're sitting in the royal blue car of my father in front of our cream colored house. I was quiet the entire ride home, attempting to form the mind-boggling questions in my head.

Guilt became Nicholas Darling as tears swelled in his eyes that mirrored my own. "You're coming of age, Sable. The truth will only break you, especially after what I did."

I do a double take, giving the man an attitude that I didn't know I held onto. "Excuse you, dad? After what you did? What did you do? Don't give me the runaround!"

Nicholas is anxious, cutting the engine off. He rubbed his hands together, darting his eyes all around; barely looking my way. "Sable, I made a promise—sealed in blood, love and sacrifice. A promise that gives your soul away to Sloan University."

"You gave my soul to Sloan University? Anyone specific?" I irritably remark, unable to blow a fuse as I tap my fingers on the dashboard of his dull, boring car.

"Amir Jones did have your soul contracted for his collection." Nicholas pipes up, causing confusion to swirl within me.

I hold up a hand, shaking my head lightly. "You're speaking in the past tense."

"I was told that his younger, half brother took your contracted soul; laying claim to it. I made this promise or deal, however, you want to look at it, in order to protect you." Nicholas gingerly explains to me.

I placed a hand to my forehead, unsure of what my father was doing. I'm starting to believe that my father is as equally as bad as his wife. "You sold my soul in order to protect me from what?"

"A powerful, vengeful, angered Witch made up of black smoke, shadows and a taste for blood." My father softly replied, hanging his head in defeat. He had me down bad, yearning to head to the gym to cry.

A rapid knock came from the passenger side on the window of the vehicle as the beautiful hues of sherbet orange and lavender made up the evening skies of Bluebell Springs. "Sae?"

River Treanor lived in the two story house of chipped, cracked, white painting with a porch out front—on our right. He had this ever-present gentle smile resting on his lips. He waved when I reluctantly cut my eyes to the blonde eighteen year old.

Before I could escape my father who gave me no real good reason as to why he sold my soul, the man called to me with sorrow present in his tone. "Dad, I don't want to hear anymore. You have ruined my future. There's no going back!"

"Sable, I wasn't done explaining anything to you. You cannot go back to Sloan University, not ever. If the Witch finds you, you'll be killed." My father warns as coldness seeps into my heart.

I nonchalantly shrug. "You didn't care before your little harlot dropped me off, so, why start caring suddenly?"

"Sable, you cannot talk about your step-mother so heinously.

CHAPTER SIX

She loves you. I'll make things right with her." My father spoke, still lacking sympathy.

I guess I know where I got my lack of emotions from which stirred a frown on my lips. I tightly squeezed the powder blue blazer. "I don't plan to go back to a school of special freaks. I can lead my life without being lumped in with a bunch of psychos. Home is where I belong."

"Sae?" River calls a second time, gaining my full attention. He taps the window once more as I unlock the door, exiting the vehicle.

My father is sitting in the driver's side, contemplating the mess that he had long created. His eyes hold tears, pricking the back of his eyes. "Your cousin, Lacey, is coming to stay with us."

Lacey Pringle was an eighteen year old who lived in South Africa. Her eyes were almond brown with lengthy, almond brown hair and olive skin. She wrote fiction books like no tomorrow with an affinity for purple just like Lila. She was slender, self conscious and a bit too oversensitive. She hadn't come to visit us since her family moved back to her hometown in Africa.

"Why is Lace coming to stay with us? This isn't a permanent fixture, yeah?" I vehemently voice, not needing another person in my life to whom I wasn't close with.

My father cupped his face before releasing a hefty sigh. "I have invited your cousin, Lacey, to live with us. It's going to be temporary. Your step-mother and I will be taking a trip on a vacation so I can discuss with her what not to teach my children."

I was barely out of the car, unto the arms of River when his words struck a chord. I didn't like what he was saying or the way he was saying his words. I do a double take, aware of the strain in his voice. "Dad, what are you holding back this time?"

My father tugged the collar of his shirt, beginning to sweat like he was hotter than the fourth of July. He had more secrets shoved up his sleeve that he was holding back. "I can't tell you all of my secrets, Sable. A good portion of them are secrets of Bluebell Springs."

"Thank you for not caring about your children enough, dad." I sharply hiss, gaining a studious look from the man.

"Sable, I care more about you than you could ever know. I'm sorry it has to be this way." My father informs me, waiting for me to slam shut the vehicle door of his.

River has this glimmer of confusion written across his face. He would be out of the know since I was just learning the many crimes of the man who claimed to love me. "What's with your dad?"

"I could tell you." I bitterly inform the blonde who is expecting a response. I want to keep the information to myself for the moment so I chew on it. I shake my head. "You wouldn't believe me if I told you, I'm not sure I even believe it."

River nonchalantly shrugs, sticking his hands into the depths of the pockets of his blue jeans. He motions towards his house with Roman sitting on the front porch, jamming out to music while Theodore Treanor was writing feverishly in what appeared to be a journal. "Would you like to come hang out with us?"

I wipe my hands down onto my black jeans, looking up at the conflicting colors of the evening skies. I wasn't sure I wanted company ever since the insanity of the day. I could use a lengthy day to myself in order to breathe properly. I was about to shut down the idea when the hazel brown eyes of Theodore widened upon seeing me.

"Sable? Good! I need an opinion!" Theodore eagerly mused, jumping up to showcase his five foot seven height. He too had mocha skin with short, chestnut brown hair and freckles galore. He was the near spitting image of Roman with a love for yellow and black flannel with yellowish tan khaki pants. He hurried over to me whereas Roman didn't budge. "Would you look at this?"

A newspaper from this evening was shoved into my hands. My eyebrows came together as River snorted from over my shoulder. "Drew Jessup was slain in his home after a dispute with an unknown assailant."

"Did his daughter ever speak to him as you suggested?" River snorts, shaking his head while touching the newspaper gently. A passive look overcame his face with his eyes becoming milky white before the blue irises returned to their natural color. His lips formed a scowl as his eyes cut to me. "Oh."

"Oh, what?" I irritably ask River, snapping my fingers upon not missing a beat of the concern in his blue eyes. I always maintained a fear of being run out of town with his eyes holding a knowing gleam.

"I had this moment like deja vu, Sae. There's nothing to worry about." River worriedly explains to me. He couldn't lie if he were about to go down with the Titanic. He lightly took a step away from me, allowing his worry and nerves to eat him alive.

"How was he murdered?" I blatantly ask, choosing to ignore River's odd behavior. I didn't appreciate the blonde acting as if I were the problem. I couldn't have killed the man nor would I have. How would the death of Drew Jessup affect me in any way, shape or form?

"Strangled to death. Somebody wanted to literally silence

him. They found this pink glowing dust at the crime scene." Theodore eagerly informs us as he taps the newspaper. He has to add an afterthought. "Gavin and I are going to solve this mystery, catch the killer and be heroes so that the ladies will love us."

Gavin Mitchell was the fifteen year old brother of Erica Mitchell and the best friend of Theodore. He was lean and lanky with tan skin, bright blue eyes, and short, golden blonde curls. He always perked up when he was around Theodore, nervous upon the mention of girls. He didn't fancy the idea of dating, especially not the opposite sex. He made it quite clear when he was thirteen while most shrugged it off, claiming he was too young to understand what he liked versus what he didn't.

"How is Gavin?" I inquire, processing the information of pink glowing dust at the scene of Drew Jessup murder. Is that why River freaked out on me? I could be on the brink of being set up by Tara, but he wants to place me at the center of the crime. I needed to change the subject, not needing another thing to get me down bad.

"He would be okay if he could get his parents to communicate with one another and him. They want to ignore him, call him a burden and shrug off his failing grades. He told me that he would speak to me when things turned around." Theodore answered, giving me a long winded explanation. He took a deep breath after, needing a second to catch oxygen in his lungs.

"When's the last time you spoke to him? It's nice to have a friend in times of great need." I gently muse to Theodore as softness infiltrates my tone. I can't feel all mushy and sappy, shaking my head as Theodore grows even more saddened.

River is holding his hands together, down in front, wanting

to put a distance between us. "I am going to check on Roman."

I rolled my candy apple green eyes as the blonde yearned to force a distance between us. What did I do to River? I focus my attention on Theodore who looks ready to have a breakdown any moment. "I apologize if I said something wrong, Theo."

"No, it's fine. I just haven't spoken to Gavin since we were thirteen. I was thinking he would come around, but it's like my best friend vanished from my life—never to be seen again." Theodore answered, allowing me a minute to realize how disconnected we had been since then. He attended Bluebell Springs High School, but I never stopped to look for Theodore; assuming he was at The Royal Torch which was the school newspaper.

"I'm so sorry, Theo. Why not reach out to him?" I mumble, garnering a thoughtful look from Theodore Treanor.

Theodore began to tap the bottom of his chin. "Only, if you'll accompany me, Sae. I haven't had a real friend in years. I haven't made the time to try outside of Gavin."

I take a minute to agree, wanting to take my mind off the current revelation and situation of Drew Jessup. I wasn't prepared to come face to face with Maria Darling at the moment, either.

Chapter Seven

I don't know how it happened, but I was in a bush on a Saturday morning; shivering from the chills gracing my slim, tanned arms. I wore my usual gray cardigan tucked into warm, black leggings that proved durable for the cooler weather. I had loose leaves of the dying bush bunched up in my hair causing my eyes to remain glossy with a scowl plastered onto my lips. I huff, hoping Theodore will hurry up with getting Gavin to open the door to face him after all the years of radio silence.

Theodore knocked on the front door of the light yellow, chipped one story house. He began to fidget, waiting for Gavin to answer with him only ever having spoken to Erica in the past two years. "Gav?"

Gavin Mitchell opened the front door with a stoic glint in his bright blue eyes. His short, honey gold curls were messy, all over the place. He was devoid of emotion, raising a blonde eyebrow at Theodore; unsure as to what his former best friend was doing at his home. "Excuse you, Theodore? Why are you on my front doorstep?"

Theodore's face fell into a habitual grimace. "I haven't seen you in forever. There's this cold case concerning Drew Jessup, father of Tara. You used to love true crime."

"I used to love things that are no longer meant for me. Can

you please leave?" Gavin spoke, pressing two fingers to the temples of his forehead; gently massaging them. He points to the bush where I'm hidden. "Take your girlfriend and get off of my property!"

"Girlfriend?! I'm friends with Erica. Or have you forgotten? You can't just exile me out of her life like you exiled me out of yours." The irritation in Theodore's voice couldn't be hidden.

I thought his irritation went beyond, straight to heartache. I was chillin' in the bush, allowing my ever growing thoughts to take precedence. I barely heard a lick of what the two began to bicker about next.

"Erica doesn't want to be your friend anymore!" Gavin sharply hissed, letting spit fly into the face of Theodore.

Theodore shook his head, blowing out a raspberry. He balled up his fist, unsure of why they had drifted apart. "Gav, I don't know what I did wrong to you!"

Gavin tugged on his short, honey blonde curls. He was stressed, mostly. "It's not what you did. It's the truth about who I have become. Can you please just go? I don't ever want to see you again and Erica told me she doesn't want to hang out with you. Your brothers are kinder to her which I can see."

Theodore worked his jawline, hurting from such an accusation. "Gavin."

The way Theodore said his name even pulled at my heartstrings, stirring heartbreak within my soul. I didn't think I could feel so bad causing me to cast my candy apple green eyes from the bush to the odd pairing of former best friends.

Gavin squeezed his eyes shut, closing the door on Theodore. He couldn't risk returning to who he no longer was.

"Are you alright?" I ask Theodore, startling the brunette lad who begged for my help—on a day, I could have been sleeping off my ever remaining exhaustion.

Theodore hung his head with a pout dancing across his lips. He begins to walk away from the front door of his best friend. "No. Why would I be? I've lost my best friend forever."

My mind briefly flashed to Roman before shaking it off, wanting not to think about his emotions. As I watched Theodore stalk off, an idea took root in my brain. I lift my hand to knock on the front door about to knock some sense into Gavin that he was evidently missing.

Gavin scowls upon reopening the front door. His bright blue eyes were no longer blue but lilac in color causing my lips to part in amazement. He was in a light gray, knit long sleeve with black jeans and black laced combat boots. Why was he wearing the same outfit in color as me? His arms become folded to his chest. "Sable Adele Darling."

"How do you know my name?" I inquire, weaving my eyebrows together. I'm too stunned to add much more as a smirk takes hold of his soft pink lips.

Gavin lightly chuckles, stepping aside while gesturing for me to enter the house. He sighed. "Erica lives with our mother. I live with our father. Come in. I'll explain everything you need to know."

My feet remained planted on the concrete of the semi stairs in front of the door. I'm not about to step foot into the possible house of a serial killer. "Nah, I'm good with waiting here for you to answer me."

"You won't find the answers you seek, standing on the front porch of my home. Outside won't show you what you seek." Gavin said, using a hand to gesture towards the inside of the house.

I'm still hesitant about stepping foot into the house of Gavin,

CHAPTER SEVEN

reluctant as one should be. I'm braver than I look, needing to start acting as such. I irritably enter the house as swirls of dark pink, dark blue and even gold bubbles infiltrate the air. A newfound surge of panic rises within me. "What's with the swirling, colorful bubbles?"

Gavin walked past me, leading me to the living room where two unsuspecting visitors were sitting, huffing out near black smoke. He sighed. "As you can see Bella and Travis are what you classify as a mirage. We can see them, they can't see us. They started appearing out of the blue when the first ever murder in Bluebell Springs in over a century took place Thursday evening."

Thursday evening is when the father of Tara Jessup had been slain in cold blood. Or in a cold strangle.

"Drew Jessup. He was the father of Tara Jessup who was quite the bully." I muse as Gavin nods.

"You and I should go visit the scene of the crime. It hasn't been touched or proofed for evidence even when his death was reported." Gavin spoke, grabbing a gold scarf, wrapping it around his neck. He handed me an icy blue scarf, gesturing for me to copy his action.

"Why are we going to see the crime scene? And, why are you wearing the same colored outfit as me? If you can't answer those then I'm heading home." I scoff, causing Gavin to force a smile onto his lips.

Gavin clasped his hands angrily together, startling me. He shook his head. "You need to see the truth for yourself, Sable even though you won't like it. As for the color matching your outfit, there's a group of us with special abilities. We always match the people who we relate to."

"If I weren't wearing any clothing then would those who

related follow suit?" I sarcastically ask, suddenly missing Roman Treanor and the close bond we once shared. I don't mean the weird, warm attraction he seemed to have for me. I meant the friendship of not expecting anything, but always being there for those who need you.

"No, Sable, that is not how our group works at all." Gavin pipes up, rolling his lilac eyes. He proceeded to inform me of more, useful information. "Your ability can change the color of your eyes; available to those with other special abilities to see but those without an ability will see those natural, candy apple green eyes."

I avert my eyes to the ground as Gavin leads me from his house, down the sidewalk, towards a stop sign. I rub my eyes at the dark purple color of the sign which is written in soft pink. I do a double take, but the purple and pink are still present. "What in the everlasting buck?"

Gavin chuckled, shaking his head. He extended his hand towards the stop sign, nodding for me to do the same. "House of Drew Jessup."

My eyebrows raise, meeting my hairline. All you had to do was say the object and name of said person to get to their joint? I was a bit amazed, but felt like it seemed familiar so I wasn't overly impressed. "Gav, you're explaining things in a backwards manner that my brain isn't processing properly."

"I apologize, Sable, but I don't have much time to explain things to you. He'll be coming to pay you a visit soon nor will you be able to avoid him. He's not as bad as everyone is making him out to be, but he can be dangerous." Gavin hissed in a whisper to me. He cut his eyes over his shoulder, making sure no one was following us.

My head grew dizzy, spinning with the teleportation of the

purple and pink stop sign. I extended a hand out to try to keep myself steady, just in case I managed to fall flat on my arse. I groan as nausea twists my stomach into a pretzel. "The younger, half brother of Amir Jones?"

Gavin averted his eyes, toying with the idea of ripping off the bandaid. He nonchalantly shrugged. "He isn't too young, Sable. He's about twenty three or twenty four so he's older than us, but younger than Amir."

"Shouldn't be surprised. The interesting ones are always out of my league." I chew on my bottom lip, partly joking. I wasn't interested in Amir's half brother any more than I was interested in dating Roman or River. I shudder at the idea, citing them as brothers in my head.

There could have been a time I saw them differently, but that was a brief flare of someone who wasn't me. I held no romantic attraction for anyone, finding it difficult to feel that way. A sad sigh fled my lips just as Gavin scoffed, leading me up to the house of Drew Jessup which had been untouched.

Dying leaves were scattered about on a perfectly manicured lawn belonging to a navy green and oak brown house. It was a rustic, rural sight; beautiful in appearance as sadness swept over me, clutching my heart tightly.

"Sable, as much as you think you can, you won't be able to turn him down. He's coming for you—not just your soul, but…" Gavin trailed off, allowing his eyes to roam over my body in anticipation that he might see something he understood the guy would fancy. He shuddered, gagging as he shook his head. "I don't see it."

I do a double take over my body. Am I that hideous to stare at? I didn't think highly of myself but my peers being put off didn't help. I could probably just go for being a serial killer.

"Gavin, can you just show me why you brought me to the house of my former bully?"

"Indeed." Gavin said, lifting a hand, allowing a shimmer of gold to come into contact with the front door, nudging it open. He led me to the garage where Drew Jessup lay; strangled to death.

I slowly approach the corpse, focused on the dark pink glowing glitterfied dust at the head of said body. I shake my head, furrowing my eyebrows. Who could have killed the man, leaving no trace, but the ability I maintained? I continue eyeing the corpse of Drew Jessup; finding no trace of blood—nothing dripping from his mouth like one would expect. "This is beyond creepy. Who could do such a thing?"

"I don't know, Miss Darling. You tell me. You are the one with a pink glowing ability. The only one in Bluebell Springs. What secrets are you hiding up your sleeve?" Gavin irritably mused, scowling as he chose to circle me like a shark in water.

Chapter Eight

One of my hands was brushing the concrete by the corpse of Drew Jessup while processing the stupid question Gavin Mitchell asked me. What does anyone's ability have to do with a cold case of murder? As my own question processes in my head, I want to slap the living daylights out of myself. Of course, I would be looked at like I was the one to do such an act. I shake my head, removing my hand while Gavin watches me intensely.

"I did not murder, Drew Jessup!" My voice is shrill as the truth is present in my voice; unclear in my body language. I stand to my full, short height just as Gavin snorts—somehow doubting the truth fleeing my dark pink lips.

"I should believe you, Sable. I'm like you, lacking emotions, but the dark pink dust tells all." Gavin sharply informs me with his nostrils flaring.

My nostrils flare just the same. I'll be damned if I'm framed or set up for a murder I didn't commit. "Pink dust proves nothing—other than that I have some type of ability. Right?"

"You can manipulate or so I'm told." Gavin reiterates what I already knew. He shrugs, about to exit the house with me following his lead.

"What are the chances that Tara is setting me up? She has always hated me, from day one." I softly suggest, gaining a snort from Gavin who was on the fence.

Gavin didn't know what he should believe versus what he shouldn't believe. He took into consideration that Tara might be setting me up. "If you can find proof that Tara set you up, I'll believe you weren't behind this."

A flicker of relief roared to life in my heart. "Where do we start?"

"Wherever your intuition leads you." Gavin scowls, once more shrugging his shoulders. It must have been his signature gesture at this point. Such an easy gesture to mimic without thinking twice about the action.

I listen to the wise words of Gavin. Wherever my intuition leads me…? I couldn't tell what that meant, struggling to be empathetic like all my classmates. "I wouldn't even know where to begin."

"You could try asking her. What's her favorite joint to chill at?" Gavin mutters, offering his help to the best of his ability. He seemed to want to get down to the matter at hand, but why? He's not the guilty one.

"Her favorite joint is The Cozy Tavern in the downtown area of Bluebell Springs. The houses were built on pine needles with stringy, pine grass by Teal Lake." I explained to Gavin who didn't look impressed nor should I have expected him to be.

Gavin took my words into consideration before his face paled. "The Cozy Tavern? Sounds familiar."

"It should. The Cozy Tavern is a popular hangout spot for cool cats like Tara, Fievel, and even Murphy." I softly muse in turn, watching sheer panic grow in his eyes.

"The two of them are founding members of Five Seconds of Winter!" Gavin squeaked, becoming pink in the face. He smoothed his hands over his face, shaking his head as shame

CHAPTER EIGHT

seemed to be his favored emotion, as of the moment.

"Murphy Thrasher is a guy." I sheepishly point out causing Gavin to harshly snort.

"No, really, Sable? I know that! So is Fievel Wong." Gavin sharply hissed with his face growing redder. He bit his tongue in the process, shortly releasing a yelp.

We were on a cold case with this blonde lunatic attempting to figure out which guy was hotter. I couldn't understand his dilemma, rolling my candy apple green eyes. "Aren't we going to need to talk to Tara about the murder of her father?"

"Actually, Sable, you will be the one to confront Tara by yourself. I didn't tell you to start world war one with the poor girl." Gavin made sure to be dramatic, draping his hand over his forehead.

"You're going to stick me with a mission that no one is going to oversee?" I inquire, up to such a challenge. I might get some time alone in order to process the hectic events that have been coming into play. I'm eighteen and shouldn't be investigating crime scenes. I would rather be at home, tuning into my favorite fictional serial killer who kills other killers, criminals, what have you.

"Sable, you are jumping the gun. I will definitely be overseeing you. There won't be a second that you'll be left to yourself." Gavin promised with doubt blooming in my heart. He walked us back to the bus stop, rubbing his hands together before a devilish smirk graced his features.

He could have been good looking, if not for the twist in his personality. He gestures for me to lay a hand on the stop sign of purple and pink. He doesn't miss the hesitation this time, with me.

"Gavin, I'm the unfeeling, cold, emphatic chick here. Everyone seems to be turning on me lately, flipping the nickel to the back." I scowl, catching Gavin shift from foot to foot.

"I'm not trying to turn on you, Sable. Talking to Fievel and Murphy could prove beneficial to your case. The fact of the matter is; you can influence Tara to come clean if she killed her father let alone if she set you up. I can't do that for you." Gavin became gentle when he spoke, but he wasn't the same Gavin from the two years prior.

I understood what broke Theodore Treanor when Gavin Mitchell refused to hear him. All this time, I thought the two friends were good—keen on listening to each other. I was wrong in more ways than one. Clearing my throat, I reluctantly placed my hand on the purple stop sign. "There's only so much a person will tell you even with my ability."

"Sae, you're just going to have to shoot for the moon and pray into the devil's butthole that it sticks." Gavin gently murmurs before he whisks us away to a different, less lively set of pine woods.

Rubbing my eyes, the dark blue building held a downward dilapidated shape with a large rectangular window on the right side. My favorite part was the hovering dark blue and dark pink cars fit for two in the red dirt parking lot. A small, barely noticeable neon sign in soft blue held the name—**'The Cozy Tavern' written** above the pine wood door.

"What's with your twisted words, Gav?" I ask as amazement causes him to part his lips. It's not my first time seeing The Cozy Tavern so I'm not that amazed, narrowing my candy apple green eyes on Teal Lake; the prettiest part.

"Nothing." Gavin said, smacking my shoulder before heading into The Cozy Tavern. He was more than enthused as I struggled to get into the building with no assistance since the

CHAPTER EIGHT

door wasn't too light.

I wring out my hands, cutting my eyes around the overflowing place with fresh baked pastries, potions, beverages, and whatnot wafting through the air. The bakery was off to the left with the counter, separating customers from the bakery. I saw caramel brown tiled flooring which bled out into the lobby with armchairs of pink and blue among coffee tables. I was reminded of a place college students would want to come chill at. Acid burns my throat from the stress my nerves chose to start producing.

Shoving it down, my eyes scan the overcrowded Cozy Tavern for the one person who enjoys making the lives of people miserable. My eyes narrow when they set on Tara, sipping on some herbal tea, laughing and joking with Murphy Thrasher and Fievel Wong. My hands find my waistline, finding the view quite unbelievable. Who laughs while their father is dead after feigning like they wanted help for their parents? I worked up the nerve to approach Tara while standing at the counter where others were sitting, chatting, laughing and doing their own thing as a whole.

Eyes piercing me keeps me rooted to my spot. I was on the brink of idly sitting down, but needed to get the truth from Tara. Has she set me up? Had she played me worse than a broken recorder competing with a fiddle? I take a few steps forward until hands pull me off to the side, out of Tara's view.

"Excuse you? I'm on a mission!" I hiss to the unassuming stranger becoming flushed with anger until cornflower blue eyes so familiar stir relief. I wave a hand at the blonde eighteen year old who is wearing a navy blue knit sweater with a darker shade of blue jeans. "I was going to get to the bottom of who killed Drew Jessup. I'm beginning to think I was set up."

River's eyes slid to Tara. His entire body was shaking as if from jitters. He must have been slamming something with caffeine. "I do not recommend testing Tara."

"Why?" I reluctantly inquire, fully examining the tall, lean, paler than usual blonde in his spot. I don't think it's caffeine, the more I stare at River. "Rivvie, are you okay?"

"I was daft enough to assume you killed Tara's dad due to the dark pink dust being at the scene of the crime so I decided to start my own investigation. I have already spoken to her." River replied in a jittery tone of shaking voice, bouncing where he gently sat on a dark blue stool. He was starting to stir worry within my heart.

I shake my head at the blonde. "How about I—?"

"No, listen, Sae. Her friend from that stupid band Roman is obsessed with slipped something in my decaffeinated, herbal, peppermint tea." River softly mused, gripping the edge of my shoulders.

"How can I help you?" I parted my lips as sadness with confusion gripped me. How could I help my friend who was profusely sweating like he was on drugs? "If I can manipulate with a special ability, do you think it's possible, I can manipulate whatever is in your system, out?"

"I don't know, Sable. I'm not sure how your ability works." River irritably says, causing an idea to float around in my brain.

I lean closer to River, pressing a finger to either side of his forehead. I concentrated on the problem at hand; yearning to strip the drug, poison or whatever was taking River by shock from his body. I heard him cough as a dark pink glow was coming from my fingertips, working to help cure the blonde which wouldn't be so simple. I frown when River leans onto the counter, coughing up a small, silver black ball. I extend a hand towards it, coating the small ball in dark pink. "I'm not sure how my special ability works either."

"It's some type of manipulation, compared to what I saw let alone what I thought I saw." River said, able to breathe easy once the killer stuff had been manipulated from his body.

"Ah, so, you have an ability?" I murmur, connecting with his cornflower blue eyes.

River scratches his short, golden blonde hair. He shrugs. "I'm more or less gifted with seeing things. I saw you kill Drew and frame Tara. I wanted to be proven wrong or that my vision is wonky."

"A Manipulator, A Seer, and what would Roman be?" I ponder, gaining a snort from River.

"A Thought Projector." River replies with a dash of a smirk lighting up his face. His blue eyes briefly turned an emerald green—the color of the walls at Bluebell Springs High School.

"I don't know if I want to call myself a manipulator though. In the real world of mortals, it's not a good thing." I irritably muse, rolling my candy apple green eyes.

"My vision was proven wrong. Tara definitely did something to her father while attempting to set you up. My tea hasn't had such a bad effect on me since my first taste of the beverage." River explained, gaining a light chuckle from me.

Chapter Nine

"I didn't mean to laugh. It just came out. I'm sorry, Riv." I softly muse, half smiling at the blonde who frowned.

"It's fine." River said, waving away my accidental burst of laughter. He didn't know what my deal was nor could I explain what was up with me.

Icy blue eyes with pale skin, short black hair, and a cold, reserved, shut off attitude belonged to a guy across the counter; eyes on us as if watching—keeping tabs.

I quirk an eyebrow in question and as a challenge. I elbow River, tearing my gaze away from the mesmerizing stranger to eye the blonde with me. "Hey, Riv! Who's…? Never mind."

"Who's what?" River was curious, following my line of vision to an abandoned beverage that looked like apple cider. He snorted. "Somebody was choosing to waste a drink."

I'm more concerned about the fact that we were being watched. Was it a testament to see if someone could finish ending River's life? I clear my throat as I choose to tell him about our stalker. "We were being watched by a guy with short, black hair, pale skin, icy blue eyes—"

"No, no, and no." River stopped me short from finishing my sentence. He even lifted up a hand, vigorously shaking his head. He seemed on the cusp of correcting me. "It sounds like you

CHAPTER NINE

were being watched, Sable."

I tilt my head to where I could give the boy a pointed look. Why is he flipping out on me so suddenly? Were there still some remnants of drugs in his system? "River—"

Taking a deep breath, the blonde did his best to become calm. He didn't fancy freaking me out but he already had. "I know a smidge about the guy after you, Sable. I am so sorry."

I didn't feel better with his words falling flat. "Does this mean you're going to leave me out to dry?"

Casting his cornflower blue eyes around The Cozy Tavern, shifting emerald green, he shook his head. "I'm taking you home before anything bad can happen. If you're seeing him then it's a matter of time before he claims you—in more ways than one. I'll try to stop him, but you're doomed."

I was nudged by River from The Cozy Tavern, catching no sign of Gavin.

However, Murphy Thrasher, took interest in our leave, choosing to follow behind us with a smirk splashed across his tanned face. His eyes were a cobalt blue with short, platinum blonde hair. He was broad shouldered with dark pink, full lips and an antagonistic smile to match. He was five foot nine, cracking his knuckles which is when the goosebumps sent shivers along my spine. His hands were buried in the depths of his pants pocket with a smugness clinging to him. "Where are you two lovebirds going?"

My mouth is sealed shut whereas River becomes tense at the off putting suggestion. I inhale sharply, keeping my calm as I face the blonde guy. "Aside from the fiery pits of Hell?"

River rolled his cornflower blue eyes to the cloudy skies of the damp seeming day. He did not want to get involved in any drama. His shoulders slump as Murphy cackles. "Don't make things worse, Sae."

"Why did you follow us out here?" I inquire as the blonde inches closer, lunging at me as if he's going to knock me out. I duck feeling the cackling pulse of my fingertips glow dark pink. My eyes burn, allowing me the comfort that they too more than likely matched the pulsating energy of my glowing dark pink fingers. Silver flashes.

"I followed you two lovebirds out here for a few reasons. I was meant to knock you out, bring you back to him then leave blondie over here for dead upon gutting him." Murphy reveals his inside information to the two of us.

I took comfort in my next action, not really planning to murder someone. I'm hesitant as the cool handle of the butcher knife in my fingers gains a shiver from me. It wasn't solely the handle that sent a wave of cold coursing down my spine, but this guy probably should have kept his mouth sealed shut. "You shall bring no harm to us."

River was prepared to fight, able to defend himself and his loved ones. His mother let him take classes revolving around martial arts, not sure what good it would do just because he was a bookworm. He read up on the subject, begging his mother to let him take on the art form. "She's right. You'll be the one gutted."

"All you would do is put a target over your head. You'll be wanted for murder, truly left for dead. Nobody would be able to help you then." Murphy cackled some more, keeping with the distraction for us.

I shake my head. "Bussy!"

Murphy punched me square in the chin, gaining even more irritation from me. His action let me plunge the knife, deep into his abdomen, burying into his gut. The cool blade sunk

CHAPTER NINE

deep within, vanishing once the five foot nine lad went down to his knees in evident pain. "What the f—?"

Pressing a pointer finger to his lips, I tutted. Didn't he know not to cuss around children? I withheld a smile as blood stained my hand from thrusting the knife into his abdomen. "We don't cuss around young adults, yeah?"

Murphy opened his mouth, allowing blood to spurt from his mouth nearly soaking my clothes. "You…what have you done?"

River tugged me back so his blood wouldn't further taint me. His cornflower blue eyes were wide, growing even more into saucers when realization slammed into him. "The knife you created became a part of him, as if he was stabbed with your imagination."

I folded my arms to my bosom, starting to believe River had lost it. "Green and blue loving, blonde, ninja wannabe, say what?"

River rolled his cornflower blue eyes once more, shaking his head before pointing to the entry point of my violence. "If you don't believe me, look for yourself."

"Any witnesses?" I hurriedly ask in a hushed whisper whereas a snort escapes River.

River cuts his eyes around, stopping on The Cozy Tavern which seems to have become invisible. He shakes his head, gently touching a hand to his ear. He was about to begin to panic when he harshly gulped, clearing his throat to remind me where we were. "We have to get you home, Sae. Don't touch anything."

I don't say another word, breathing uneasily as I allow River to pull me from my own crime scene. I had become a murderer with a joy for the action of removing trash such as Murphy from the universe. I'm not aware of River making us leave but he does, getting us to our block in no time flat. "Well…"

River held in a puff of air, shaking his head. "Sable, don't start."

"I wasn't a murderer before Tara's fathers death." I softly muse, wiping cold sweat from my fingers down onto my black leggings. I see the alarm surface in his cornflower blue eyes. "I'll shower as best as I can."

"You do that, Sae. Not that it will absolve you of the crime you committed with me. How can I be sure now that you didn't kill her father?" River is fully panicking, pacing in front of me even after we reach the step of my front door. He looks so cute in panic mode as something warm bursts to life in my chest.

Acid once more burns the back of my throat as excitement has flourished in my veins. Could River have made me feel such a warm, fuzzy feeling? Massaging the temples of my forehead, not wanting it to be so. "River, I didn't kill her father. You've known me for years!"

"Yes. I have known you for years, Sable! People knew Dexter Morgan for years! And, look what happened?!" River groaned, shaking his head while tugging at his blonde hair.

How else could I comfort the boy? I clear my throat to gather his attention. When he stops pacing, I inch closer, cupping his face upon standing on my tippy toes. "I wouldn't purposely kill anyone. Have you learned nothing from all of the years of us growing up together?"

River's eyes searched mine, neither of us, having realized my left hand was still bloody from stabbing Murphy in the abdomen. He did the most ridiculous thing by pressing his lips to mine in a gentle, feverish, hot manner. He kissed me, shocking me for a change since the blonde was usually well put together. "I do know you, Sable. You are the disconnected,

CHAPTER NINE

emphatic loner with no remorse for anyone else even your kiss tells as much."

Hurt, if you could call it that, clutched my heart from his last sentence. I opened my mouth to protest, to correct the blonde when the front door of the house squeaked open. A giddy squeak came from the cousin I craved to disown who was the same age as us. "River, this is Lacey Pringle—the cousin."

River Treanor extended a hand to the olive hand of Lacey who was five foot three, slender with almond brown eyes, long flowing, almond brown hair. "Lacey, it is so nice to meet you. Will you be attending Bluebell Springs High?"

"I will be attending Bluebell Springs High!" Lacey eagerly informed River, glad to shake his hand. In all of her life, she hadn't met the cute blonde who broke my barely feeling heart within seconds of her returning to my life. She didn't know the pain he caused me right before her appearance.

I don't hate Lacey, but she was always so chipper, outgoing and positive. It hurt my soul for how organic sunshine the eighteen year old from South Africa was. I could tell I was probably viewing her wrong, wanting to give my cousin the benefit of the doubt. "One thing I vaguely recall about Lace, she's a writer of sports romance with a splash of mystery horror on the side."

Lacey grinned like no tomorrow. "Most people forget, not caring. I'm looking to publish my debut novel while living in Bluebell Springs with you, Sae."

"There is plenty to see in order to inspire a new work." I muse to Lacey as an idea lights up the cornflower blue eyes of River.

River had been listening intently to our conversation, mostly staring at Lacey with a fast growing fondness. He was making the pain in my chest grow, but did he care? He was good at making those around him seen only to be shunned soon after. "How about you, me, Sae, Roman, Theo, Gav and Erica get together to hangout at Fazbear's Kitchen?"

My stomach growled at the infamous pizza place. I remember the arcade games with a sleek, black marble counter for the adults in the front to sit and drink. There were booths in the arcade for us teenagers to chill, but we hadn't been to Fazbear's Kitchen in ages. They were the best pizza in Bluebell Springs, located on the outskirts of the town; separated from the rest of our favorite joints. "Haven't been there in years."

River fiddled with his ear, giving me a funny glance. "Oh, really? I thought we went years prior until the scare…"

Lacey was curious, parting her lips while waiting for River to finish his sentence. She waved it off when the blonde trailed off. "I would love to hangout with you all! This is going to be an exciting change of pace."

"You can even tell us what your debut novel is about so we can get ready to buy it." River said with stars in his eyes. He would fall for her, for her books. He was the town bookworm after all, but he wasn't the only reader in Bluebell Springs.

Chapter Ten

My spine shuddered, pressed into the wall of the faded soft blue walls blended into green. I was leaning up against the wall, watching my friends in the arcade of Fazbear's Kitchen after all these times. A bitterness clung to my dark pink lips, especially realizing what River did to me. I should have pieced together why I was so messed up long ago, but how could I? I was in a raven colored leather jacket over a black tee shirt, tucked into a pink mini skirt with gray stockings.

I had nothing else to wear but the outfit had been posed on my bed as if picked out. My father had taken my step-mother out of Bluebell Springs to give the woman a stern talking to. I highly doubted he would have picked out such an outfit. Nor could Lacey have done it since she had been too busy daydreaming about River. I was so tempted to plunge my fingers into my ears, because she wouldn't stop yapping about the swoon worthy blonde next door who was the exact same age.

I probably should have congratulated my cousin but found it lackluster to care. My mind needed to focus on the mysteries looming over my head like a dark cloud. My lips become pursed as the feeling of being watched takes hold of me. In hindsight, I could have just gone home; giving me nothing to do but crave the dangers of a new adventure in order to discover the killer of Tara's father. I was beginning to believe I had killed Drew Jessup, most especially after accidentally slaying the likes of Murphy Thrasher.

My candy apple green eyes shift to the left, catching sight of my stalker or so that's what River yearns to believe. I raise a challenging eyebrow at the glass mug of yellow liquid. So, my stalker was an alcoholic? The tiny hairs on my neck rose when he appeared next to me, leaning into the wall, lifting the mug to his lips. "Um, why, are you…?"

"Stalking you?" His voice held a smidge of amusement, sounding dead, monotone even. He was wearing a light blue denim jacket over a navy blue tee shirt with light blue denim jeans. His slick, black hair remained parted so his icy blue eyes could capture every scenario before him.

I purse my lips. "I didn't use that term. You did."

"I'm Jesse." He nonchalantly spoke, shrugging as if it were no big deal. He extended the drink towards me. "It's cream soda. Some of us have a low tolerance to more adult beverages so we can't stomach them."

I shake my head at the stranger who is leaning awfully close to me. I get a whiff of the cream soda, proving the vanilla scented liquid to be true on his part. I catch a chuckle falling from his lips while curiosity remains clutching my heart. "I'm Sable."

"Well, Sable, it's nice to officially meet you." Jesse said, lifting his free hand for me to shake. His icy blue eyes held a dare while an invisible blush found its way to my olive features. He's got this aura of resistance about him.

I bite my tongue, eyeing his hand as if being compelled to do so. I scowl at myself, knowing nothing good could come of conversing with a stranger; especially one stalking me. If Jesse was as bad as River said then there was no point in allowing myself to get slapped into harm's way. "I wish I could say the same, but you must mean harm to me."

"You're going off of what you've recently heard. You don't know me." Jesse said, setting his drink down onto the counter top. He had this annoyed stare clinging to him in doing so.

I carefully observe Jesse, raising an eyebrow as Jesse refocuses his icy blue gaze on me. "Exactly, but why would I want to get to know somebody who thinks my soul is theirs to steal let alone keep? Life doesn't work like that."

Wiping a hand down his face, Jesse shakes his head with this incredulous look plastered across his face. He doesn't know what to make of his current predicament. "I'm sorry, Sable, but you must have confused me with someone else. I did not steal your soul. My half brother has your contracted soul, planning to do terrible things with it."

Processing the information was a short circuit to my brain. I couldn't be sure he was telling the truth. "You more than likely are lying. My father would have told me if it was your brother."

An idea surfaced in his icy blue eyes as confusion swept into them. Jesse furrows his eyebrows. "So, where is your father? Can he confirm or deny as we speak?"

"He went on vacation with his young wife." I softly muse, averting my candy apple green eyes to the floor of Fazbear's Kitchen.

Jesse chewed the inside of his cheek, nodding before thinking it wise to add his two cents. "Interesting. He tells you a partial truth and abandons you. He really doesn't know what he's doing, leaving you unprotected, unguarded."

I shiver in despair, thrilled at the mere idea of the conversation dying. I shudder as I briefly glare in Jesse's direction. "Just leave me alone, will ya?"

"Sable, it's too late to shut me out. You opened the door by speaking first. I cannot leave you nor will I." Jesse vehemently spoke, returning to his drink on the counter. There was something really concerning about the twenty three year old causing me to keep my eyes on him.

I wanted to get back to my friends who were scattered around the arcade, playing whichever game struck their fancy. My eyes found River playing some racing game whereas Roman and Theodore were foosballing. My candy apple green eyes slid around the area in search of my cousin who was sitting at our booth, feverishly writing in a notebook like her life depended on it. "I'm chilling with my friends."

"Our friends." Jesse teased with a smirk becoming transparent on his face. He was okay smiling, reminding me of a budding serial killer. He slung an arm around my shoulders once he grabbed his cream soda, leading me in the direction I was staring. He forced my hand, plopping us in front of Lacey who didn't bother to glance up.

His arm around me was warm and comforting. I almost let myself fall into the trap of the touch, shuddering since it shouldn't feel safe. He was way too old, right? He was whom I had been warned about via my loved ones. Why did I have this sinking feeling that my father wasn't telling me everything?

"Lace!" I hiss as Jesse slams half of the cream soda, reminding me of someone who couldn't sit still even when he was sitting still. I snap my fingers, finally irritating my oblivious cousin enough for her to stop writing.

"WHAT?!" Lacey angrily roared, slamming her pen down onto her notebook. She took to being distracted very badly, wanting to snap the necks of those who dared interrupt her. When she was on a roll, in her own space, zoned out—you did not fancy messing with the fire-breathing dragon that would take place.

Jesse winced beside me, clearing his throat, gaining her attention. His action caused her flaring nostrils to slow, dying down. "I'm Jesse. You must be the cousin of Sable."

Lacey let her heart rate slow to normal as her eyes were darting back and forth. Her mind was swirling with worry, doubt, and enthusiasm. "Y-yes, you must be the demon spawn of shadows that we were all warned about. Nice to meet you."

"Demon spawn of shadows? There's a first." Jesse lightly chuckled, extending a hand towards Lacey in order for her to shake. In doing so, he held up a finger before adding onto his original thought. "I'm not some demon spawn of shadows. I'm not evil either."

I don't think I'll be able to breathe until Jesse has disappeared into the night. My evening had been going well enough, grunting once River plopped down into the seat next to me, shoving me closer into the side of a highly amused Jesse. "River, why, so sour?"

Lacey rolled her almond brown eyes. "He lost his stupid racing game. You're eighteen, River Treanor; those games don't matter anymore."

Warmth spread through me, continuing to grow while pressed into Jesse. He didn't seem to mind or care as his arm lingered around my torso. "Games tend to help us guys unwind, Lace."

Lacey became flushed as River grew anxious, tilting his head in our direction. "Oh yeah, River, this is Jesse."

"The evil who owns the soul of Sable?" River nearly stutters, the question falling from his lips.

"He's not evil." Lacey disregards the assumption of the blonde, recalling the earlier words of Jesse. She shoots him a small smile, more welcoming than most would be; especially the residents of Bluebell Springs.

"Lace is correct. I'm not evil or some demon spawn. I don't own Sable's soul, just because we share a deep, profound connection—" Jesse is smirking with those words until the bickering of Roman and Theodore approaching us interrupts his unfinished sentence. He's intrigued by the younger brothers of River.

I'm just sitting quietly, thankful not to have to chime in for a change while I take it all in. I see the tension in River after Jesse's words barely soothe the blonde boy.

"I am not a sore loser!" Roman hisses to a smirking, laughing Theodore.

Theodore pokes the cheek of his middle brother. "You are definitely a sore loser, Roro."

"Theo, you want to keep those hands of yours, right?" Roman challenges, practically hissing at his younger brother. He stops in front of the booth where River, Lacey, Jesse and I are sitting. His light gray eyes drink us all in, stopping on Jesse. "What's with the monster clinging to Sable?"

I tense up, watching the white hot rage flash to the surface in Roman's eyes. I knew all too well how this was going to go. I don't get a word in edgewise as River groans out loud, choosing to speak up.

"This is Jesse. Jesse, this is Roman and Theodore; they are my idiot brothers." River made the introductions brief, keeping Roman as unhappy as could be.

"Why are you bothering, Sable? She's with me!" Roman wasn't simply scowling at Jesse; he was full on glaring at the twenty three year old. He raked his hands through his hair,

CHAPTER TEN

watching Jesse form a response.

"Sable, how come you didn't tell me you were with him?" Jesse asked while a Cheshire grin took hold of his pale features. He was feigning shock with a splash of dramatics. He shook his head, placing his head to his hand on the table.

"I'm not with anybody. Plain and simple. I don't have time for relationships that are beyond platonic." I irritably groaned, causing Roman to snort.

Roman made hand gestures, managing to whack Theodore in the face by mistake. "Then, what is this? You two look quite cozy. You actually look like you're ready to marry the guy, Sable!"

River cleared his throat, shaking his head. He was about to make his brother think differently. "I don't think so, Roman. Stop jumping to conclusions!"

"Why, Riv? Actions speak louder than words!" Roman angrily voiced, before storming off. He was good at being a typical teenage boy, forgetting how girls mature before boys. He was hurt beyond recognition, having assumed I was his; his entire world.

River pardoned himself from the table in order to chase Roman down, allowing Theodore to sit down in his spot.

A frown clung to my dark pink lips while my candy apple green eyes flickered to the table. I just wanted to get down to the bottom of who killed Drew Jessup. Was the murder a one time thing or were more going to start taking place?

Chapter Eleven

I was sitting at the kitchen counter at home, starting to comprehend the meaning of loneliness. After everyone met Jesse the month prior at Fazbear's Kitchen; we all went our separate ways. I barely spoke to Roman and River who wouldn't even look at me while walking to and from Bluebell Springs High. I had become invisible to those who meant the most to me. I hadn't seen or spoken to Jesse, making me wonder if he wasn't a figment of my imagination.

The colder months were upon us causing me to make some peppermint flavored hot chocolate, delighting my taste buds. My cousin had been stuck in her bedroom the entire duration of her stay so far. How could I be this bad at people-ing in over a month? I didn't bother to reach out to those choosing to ignore me, figuring it was for the best. A sigh fell from my dark pink lips as I blew on the peppermint hot cocoa some more.

Eager knocks came from the front door causing me to snort. Who could be bothering me at such an early hour on a weekend? I take a few sips from the hot chocolate, not yearning to move from my spot where my butt is planted. I sigh, hearing the bedroom door of cousin Lacey swish open. I feel her presence before she speaks from over the counter, leading down the hall where all the bedrooms and the bathroom resided.

CHAPTER ELEVEN

"Are you going to get that? What if it's your boyfriend?" Lacey taunts with her almond brown eyes holding a spark of aggression that I had missed before.

I gently press my palm on the table, frowning at my hot chocolate. I remove myself from the light brown oak, stool made chair. I cut her a sharp glare. "It shouldn't be me getting the door, always. What if it's a suitor for you?"

"I have been here for a sole month, Sae. It's not for me. When I start paying bills for my share of the rent then and only then, will I answer your precious door. As is, I'm a busy writer with little to no time on my hands." Lacey hissed as callous and rude as could be.

Her nostrils were flaring like a witch from a storybook—meaning a hooked nose, green in the face with a monstrous envy that shouldn't exist. Her dark pink lips were pressed into a hard line when she went swishing back into her bedroom.

I slowly, but surely tugged open the front door to find who I would rather not have found.

A smile of unease sits on his lips as he's holding a beige envelope in his palms, gesturing to it. He's five foot nine; lean and lanky, as to be expected from a Witch burning with anger and darkness. His icy blue eyes held excitement. "Congratulations!"

I shrug. "Congratulations, on what? I'm not attending Sloan University! There was no proper submission since my stepmother has lost her brain cells."

His teeth were showing as he became pink faced. He points to the envelope. "Who is Lila Darling?"

"My sister." I irritably reply, gingerly taking the beige envelope from his hands. I could be rude to Jesse, but what good would that do me? I step aside to allow him to enter the kitchen of the one bedroom, attic based house. I return to my place at the counter in front of my hot chocolate, ignoring the cream marble flooring with cream painted walls.

My father and step-mother thought it a good idea to have a minimalistic home. They didn't believe in 'freedom of expression, not a good impression' in their home. As many times as Lila and I tried to convince them otherwise, they just wouldn't hear us out.

"Oh." Jesse said, making a face as if to say 'yikes' while tugging on the collar of his navy blue tee shirt underneath his light blue denim jacket. He nonchalantly shrugged. "It's a wedding invite."

"A wedding invite?" My head begins to swirl with disbelief at those words. I hurriedly checked the envelope, encrusted in lilac and dark pink. "Lila Darling and Simon Blackthorn are pleased to cordially invite you to their December 25th wedding."

"What's wrong, Sable? Why do you look so stressed and flushed as if the end of the world has struck you?" Jesse lightly teases, calculating my facial expressions. He can see the wheels turning in my head.

Embarrassment becomes my best friend, appearing on my face. I didn't know my sister was going to marry Simon Blackthorn! I take a few deep, sturdy breaths. "Simon Blackthorn is two years older than Lila! She's too young to be married."

"Actually, that depends. How long have they been dating?" Jesse disagrees, slick in his responses which make me just want to slap him silly.

I'm on the verge of ripping out my thick, maple brown curls when something occurs to me. I love my sister, but as time went on; we grew apart. "If Lila wants to marry a stranger then

CHAPTER ELEVEN

that's her choice. She may be twenty, but she's an adult, right? Who should care?"

Becoming disturbed by my utter lack of concern for Lila, Jesse vehemently frowns. He scoffs, rolling his icy blue eyes to the roof of the kitchen, shaking his head. "She's your sister. You should definitely care about what happens to her. No one was saying that, but by law; she's an adult—has been since she became eighteen."

Anger bubbles under the surface of my skin, yearning to boil over. I want to stab Jesse, but he hadn't said anything far fetched let alone untrue. I need to get my temper in order before I'm thrown into the Bluebell Springs Institution. Shaking out my hands, I nod in agreement with Jesse. "Sure, she's an adult."

"Did you even read the full invitation?" Jesse said, touching his hand to the one I held the letter in. His touch was warm, generating a buzz I didn't want—couldn't want. He proceeded to tap my fingers and the letter. "Before you continue jumping to conclusions, try reading the full letter. Simon is a good…well, decent enough guy."

I ignored those last words, reading the last bit of the letter. I felt like a complete fool as relief swarmed my heart, putting me at ease. Tension still zapped the atmosphere causing me to slowly remove my hand from under his, blushing like no tomorrow. I clear my throat. "Why exactly have you shown up on my doorstep?"

"Why do you think, Sable?" Jesse scoffed, rolling his eyes with a smirk clinging to his lips. He tapped the letter. "I figured this was as good a time as any to start."

"Excuse you? Start, what?" I'm skeptical while the question flies from my lips.

Jesse leans closer, grinning as he chooses to lightly tap my nose, sending shivers down my spine. His grin never once wavered, especially with the next words he chose to lay on me. "This wedding will prove as good as any time to start courting the future Mrs. Jesse Wick."

My lips part in disbelief. "Um, excuse you? Do you see any partakers in your disillusioned fantasy?"

Extending a hand to my arm, Jesse stroked the vein causing the surge to melt into him overcome me. He must have some type of manipulation or controlling ability. Otherwise, how could I suddenly be weak in the knees for a stranger that you didn't take home to dad? He furrows his dark eyebrows, expectantly. "The choice is yours, Sable. I'm not going to force you, but what we have is electric and will grow as time goes on."

I begged to differ, leaning back while moving my arm from the counter top altogether. I assumed I would be good with just leaving it out of reach of the Witch. "You are so delusional, my good, sir."

"Denial is the first step, but that's okay. You've already got tingly sparks shooting through your body for me. I'm not stupid or blind to body language, Sable." Jesse softly muttered, walking over to the front door. He was about to leave me breathless as something seemed to click in the back or his mind. "Tell your…sorry, our friends, I say, hi."

I'm watching his every move as he winks before disappearing out the front door. I'm one hundred percent sure he knows that my friends have ditched me prior to the previous month. I had been itching to get into contact with them, but every fiber of my being went against it. I get up, peeling open the front door to beautiful, wintery flavored skies making me shiver some more. The sun is so bright, it's nearly blinding until River and

CHAPTER ELEVEN

Erica appear in my view.

"What's up, y'all?" I ask the question in my mind as excitement floods my body. I feel different, slightly changed, more energetic and down to do things other teenagers did, suddenly.

River scoffs, cutting his eyes to the wheelchair bound Erica in white and pink. He was wearing a dull, emerald green sweater with checkered pants to match. He was definitely going for the whole nerd getup. "Lila sent us a wedding invitation. Do you know the guy?"

"Does she know the guy?" Erica posed the question that had surfaced in my head.

Alas, I didn't want to talk about the sudden wedding of my big sister. I needed to change the topic, doing something different. "How about we not talk about weddings which are for much more mature adults?"

"Sure." Erica agreed with River who simply nodded.

River seemed uncomfortable as if I were on a list of sworn enemies that he was keeping. He tapped his wristwatch. "I do have to go, but we should hang out sometime. We were thinking of taking a camping and hike trip to Mount Venus for a good week or so. Would you like to join us, Sable?"

"What about Lacey? I'm sure it would be refreshing for her to leave that bubble she's doused herself in." I softly muse, half joking as I jab a thumb over my shoulder, towards the house.

River harshly gulped, vigorously nodding. "Lacey should come so invite her and that boyfriend of yours! This way, we can get to know each other some more."

"We also want to make sure that Jesse is no threat to you. We've been told so many scary stories about him." Erica gently explains with her voice coming off clipped which was normal for her when she spoke. She liked to think she was always right, arguing with even the strangest of people. She could be proven wrong and still not want to see it.

"He's no threat to me." I speak feeling myself flush. He's not a threat to me, but my sexuality of inexperience is a different story. I keep those words repressed, not needing the weight to burden anyone let alone me in the long road.

"Roman will be there." River blurted as if that should scare me off from reconnecting with my friends. His cornflower blue eyes widened as if he spoke something into existence that shouldn't be spoken. "I am so sorry…"

"Why are you sorry? Roman is your brother." I gently remind the blonde while Erica watches our exchange in silence.

River does a double take, shrugging. "I assume you would be upset since Roman and you are on bad terms."

"He's still holding a grudge?" I raise an eyebrow while River gulps before slowly nodding.

"I'm sorry, Sae. He is so ticked off with you." River murmurs with guilt and shame surfacing in his cornflower blue eyes.

"I don't see where I did anything wrong, but okay." I softly muse, shrugging off the concern River felt on behalf of Roman's disgust towards me. I knew the day would bloom when my former best friend walked away from me for good. I just didn't know when the day would be.

Chapter Twelve

"Hydration is the key to not being so moody." River informs Roman and Theodore while his middle brother just rolls his eyes. He's chirping away to them on our way to the school assembly as an idea sears to life in the back of my brain.

I wanted to talk to Roman, hoping he would forgive me for upsetting him. I was tagging along with the Treanor brothers while being given the silent treatment. Their mother didn't raise them to be as rude as they were being. "Roman, can I talk to you?"

Roman's body tensed, becoming gifted with unease. His light gray eyes didn't bother to even flick my way. His jaw was set, working it into the ground allowing the sorrow within to nearly bury me alive. "We're at school, Sable!"

"Roman!" I refrained from hiding the urgency in my tone, watching him slightly hesitate to finish following his brothers into the gym. I lift up my fingers, wrapping a hand softly around his wrist. I tug him in the opposite direction, needing some privacy to profusely apologize for the pain I'd caused him.

Roman blows a raspberry, folding his arms to his chest whenever we are alone in an empty classroom brokering a set of chills from the both of us. He quirked an eyebrow. "Sae, what exactly do you want? The school assembly is equally as important as anything else at Bluebell Springs."

My eyes search his as something swells in my heart. "Roman, I didn't—"

Roman shakes his head, scoffing at me. "Sae, don't add onto whatever is going through your brain. We've been best friends since childhood. I know in your own twisted, disturbing way that you care about me."

"I didn't plan for some guy to act like he owns me. I didn't mean to hurt you either." I reply with regret and pain evident on my face.

Roman calculates me from head to toe, processing my words. His light gray eyes have this gleam to them. "Sable, you are my entire world. I'm lost without you. You can't just choose some stranger over me."

I moved closer to Roman, placing my hands on either side of his shoulder. My eyes held honesty intermingling with sincerity. "I did not choose some stranger over you. There's this magnetic attraction that I'd rather not have towards Jesse Wick."

Roman is still hurt, keeping his arms crossed to his chest. His blue leather jacket clung to his mocha skin with pursed pink lips. He could be a dream for the right one. "It's due to him owning the contract to your soul. I'm sure we could get it back."

"You would want me to get my soul back even if I break your heart?" I ask the dumbest question possible as he scoffs. I see a barely visible smile lingering in his light gray eyes.

Roman cuts his eyes to the ground before he shakes his head. "There's no way you would want some older guy if he didn't hold the contract."

"How could you know that? What if it isn't on account of the contract?" I ask with a tremble in my voice. I wasn't sure if I was scared but Roman gave a slight nod of the head, proving that I was indeed scared of it being a reality.

"Sable, you are definitely scared. I don't blame you." Roman softly muttered, leaving me with no other choice.

I take him by surprise, taking myself by surprise just the same when I press onto my toes, gently placing a kiss to his lips. A spark of warmth with hope ignited as his eyes fluttered closed. "I…"

Roman coughed before his lips met mine, peaking a fever. His hand wound up in my hair as I allowed it to transpire. His lips move in sync with mine, proving we could be a perfect match. "Sable, I love you. I've been in love with you forever."

The steam of the kiss dwindled, dying as quick as the heat began. My heart dropped as my anxiety fluttered to life. I place one of my hands to the one he had in my hair, shaking my head at him. "How could you love me?"

"It's simple, I just can. You mean the world to me. Nothing will ever change that." Roman whispered, pressing his face into the top of my head.

My maple brown curls were a mess as confusion made itself known in my heart. I was meant to be uncaring, cold, asinine, shut off from my peers. I was right in my earlier emotion towards Roman even with the brief flicker of warmth shared; we wouldn't be more than friends. Fear of rejection grew in me, knowing that Roman wouldn't agree. "I'm not in love with you."

"It's the contract that Jesse owns—once you get it from him, you'll see. You don't want him in the way you may think." Roman said, pressing a kiss once more to my head of maple brown curls.

I'm panicking as I shake with fear, blending with nerves. I

can't agree with him. "I'm sorry, Roman."

"Don't be, Sable. We are going to fix this." Roman promises, trying to cling to me like a kid clinging to their parents in a name brand store of strangers.

Tears prick the back of my eyes. After the back and forth, I was able to finally come to a conclusion. I could not pretend to be happy with Roman, only to sit idly by. I couldn't pretend to be happy with River; if the blonde came out to ask it of me. Shaking my head, I remove myself from Roman who furrows his eyebrows at my action. "Roman, I don't want you as more than a friend."

Roman doesn't move closer to me. His light gray eyes, drink me in from head to toe. He remains leaning into the desk with which he's at. He couldn't hide the sorrow or bear the thought of losing me. "Sable, if we can get the contract back…"

"Roman, if we can get the contract back I still won't love you as more than a best friend. In fact, you could be my brother, so could River and Theodore. This has nothing to do with my soul being sold to an angry, barely harmful Witch!" I sharply hiss, hoping Roman would finally hear me out.

Roman averts his eyes to the floor, torn on how to feel. He could tell it was unholy to ask more from me. He was wrong in assuming he knew my feelings even if he could **Thought Project**. He came to his senses, slowly nodding his head. "Okay, I won't press my luck and ruin our friendship."

"Thank you, Ro." I softly muse, aware of how difficult it was for the seventeen year old stud. I'm sure someone else could help him forget about me; after all, there was a particular blonde girl who had her eyes on him. A half smirk bounces onto my lips. "How about Erica Mitchell?"

"Let's not further discuss romance." Roman ground his teeth

CHAPTER TWELVE

as something else was on his mind. He was curious about whether we had discovered who killed Drew Jessup. He was informed by River and Theodore whereas Gavin had finally spoken to his best friend after all the years of distance between them. He tilted his head to the side, yearning to find a way to best pose the question on his mind. "Did you figure out who set you up?"

My candy apple green eyes caught the glance of icy blue eyes holding disappointment before my eyes shifted to Roman. I had been staring off into the distance before watching Jesse appear in black smokey shadows, reminding me of blackbirds. I was curious about his appearance until the disappointment in his eyes reached me. I took it to mean that he knew about the brief, meaningless kiss I exchanged with my best friend since childhood. "No."

"It was more than likely Tara. Gavin told me he met Fievel Wong and Murphy Thrasher." Roman voiced, causing Jesse's interest to pique. He jumped when Jesse walked into view, clearing his throat. He didn't get spooked easily, usually the one to do the startling on behalf of our peers.

"Fievel Wong and Murphy Thrasher? My father was friends with Drew Jessup, so I vaguely recall seeing his brat of a daughter." Jesse made sure to keep his icy blue eyes focused on Roman, choosing to ignore me even when he was approximately within seconds of grazing me.

Holding my breath, my curiosity grows. I tilt my head only to shake it once my brain catches up to whatever is being said. "Why are you asking about two quarters of Five Seconds of Winter?"

"Fievel and Murphy are bad news. I know them, personally." Jesse keeps his back turned to me causing me to shudder since he knew exactly what he was doing. He was pissed at me nor could he make his anger any clearer.

"I'm sordidly disappointed. I assumed Five Seconds of Winter were all girls—our age." Roman is blushing, casting his eyes from around Jesse to me. He would often tell me about his crush on the faceless, animated Fievel who from their videos of animation were a set of five girls nor did their voices prove different.

Jesse chuckled, sucking in a sharp air of breath. "If you like guys—"

"NO!" Roman angrily roared, wanting to hunt the band members down to snap their necks. He had been lied to, betrayed, touching himself to a male the entire time without knowing. He tried to force his anger under control but his nostrils were dead set on flaring. "I like girls! Being homosexual is wrong, a sin, and will have you pitching a tent while burning in the fiery depths of Hell!"

"It's the Underworld, Treanor!" Jesse sharply, corrected, rolling his icy blue eyes at Roman while shaking his head in disagreement. "I'm fairly certain the term you are looking for is called, being gay or bi. Also, it's only criminals, rapists, assaulters and such who have to pay for their crimes in the afterlife."

"How do you know this?" I softly inquire, lifting an eyebrow with Jesse copying my action, but having yet to disclose the full truth.

"I'll speak to you alone. As for you, Roman, it'll be okay. Fievel isn't so much the problem as happens to be Murphy who influences bad decisions amongst their group." Jesse reveals, gaining a sigh from me even when it clicked that I had killed Murphy; recent events made me forget until that moment.

CHAPTER TWELVE

Roman's eyes are darting back and forth as he's having a full blown panic attack. He bends over, placing his hands on his knees. He seems unable to breathe as he tugs at his hair. "Is that why Theodore and Gavin would laugh at me? They knew?"

"Roman, sexuality isn't important as we speak. Murphy Thrasher could very well know the truth about the murder of Drew." Jesse mumbled as Roman headed for the exit of the vacant classroom.

"I'm going to tell River and Theodore that we're forming a group effort to get Murphy to talk." Roman scoffs, rolling his light gray eyes as he exits the classroom with disbelief still present within. His mind was blown. Who could blame him?

I too would be disturbed if I discovered the band I had been listening to for years turned out to be the opposite sex. I'd be less pressed about it since it's not like anything would happen with them in real life. I forgot I'm alone with Jesse until the twenty three year old clears his throat, just to remind me. "What's with the disappointment in me? I've done nothing to or against you."

Jesse kept a steady gaze on me before a thick, piece of white page appeared in a lick of blue flames in one hand. "This is the contract for your soul which isn't worth having, as it turns out."

"I killed Murphy Thrasher in self defense." I mumble in response to Jesse who smirks. I'm too dazed to pay him any more attention. My green eyes set on the contract with hope spreading in my heart.

"Did you really kill him?" Jesse asked with a knowing glint in his icy blue eyes that I failed to notice. His words went right over my head as a whole.

Chapter Thirteen

My eyes widen upon me rubbing at them as my lips part with confusion. "My soul isn't worth having?"

A knowing glint is present in his icy blue gaze. He allows me to briefly peer at the contract that did hold my soul prisoner. "I don't want your soul anymore, Sae. You have proven a liability, especially with my heart."

"It was a meaningless kiss that needed to happen." I irritably voice, rolling my candy apple green eyes. I can see the disconcert in his eyes as he wiggles the contract in front of me.

Jesse set his icy blue eyes on the contract, allowing bright blue flames to destroy it. He nonchalantly shrugs as the ever-present frown returns to take precedence on his lips. "I don't own your soul anymore, Sable. No one does, so you cannot blame others for your actions or words."

My heart beat with sadness, excitement and a splash of anxiety. I had my freedom or so my soul did as tears remained present in the back of my eyes. "Thank you, Jesse."

"I didn't just destroy the contract for you or me. I wanted to prove something to your friends, family, and my overbearing father. He doesn't control me, no one does." Jesse pipes up causing my eyebrows to knit in unison.

CHAPTER THIRTEEN

"Who is your father?" I gently ask, forgetting about the assembly at Bluebell Springs High. I was already too involved in the mystery afoot.

Jesse folds his arms to his chest, leaning into the wall of the classroom. He looked torn on explaining who his father was. He sighed, choosing to rip the bandaid off. "I'm the son of Hades. My mother was a Dark Witch; his first, unnatural, slain love."

My heart fluttered via his words. "Did he kill her?"

"Yes, my father killed my mother—for her soul. His true love will always be Persephone or something along those lines. I tuned the God of the Underworld out after he blatantly admitted to murdering my mother." Jesse said, sucking in a sharp air of breath. His confession hit like a ton of stone bricks weighing down a boat in the sea.

"Have you been on the run or…?" I trail off in an attempt to squeeze more information from the man.

"I haven't been on the run from my father. I have been living in plain sight. He knows where I am, even insisting on me helping Amir with Sloan University." Jesse said, shuddering at the sheer idea of doing what his father wanted.

"Why?" I scoff, believing the God of the Undead to be as evil as his namesake. I see Jesse chew on his bottom lip in contemplation before averting his icy blue eyes to the ground of the classroom. "I assume your father is evil like any and all Greek Mythological beings."

"You're straining yourself on the wrong words. As far as I'm concerned, my father is evil for killing my mother, but he has tried to change which is why he's tried to convince me to help Amir with Sloan University." Jesse grumbles, shaking his head.

I didn't think the name was a good fit either, but that didn't mean to knock it. I cough to gain his attention, watching reluctant blue eyes trail up to meet my candy apple green ones. "I get that you think it's a stupid idea, but there are those with uncontrolled abilities who could use the help."

"You included. You just don't want to accept the help." Jesse said as I strode over to be next to him. He sighed, pressing his fingers to the temples of his forehead. "My father will be out for my head after destroying your soul contract. Do me a favor and return to Sloan University where you'll be protected."

"Jesse—?" I had just drawn closer to Jesse when he shot me a glare of daggers that chilled me to the bone.

"If any other guy touches you, I will put them six feet under. I'll be seeing you, Babygirl." Jesse softly muttered before disappearing in a swirl of black ravens with a splash of blue flames. He was exactly who he said he was, leaving ice to douse my heart. He could have stayed to further explain, leading me to snort.

If he's on the run then how will he know who touches me or not? I shake off the thought of jealousy and romance becoming startled once a particular blonde pops his head in the door. "River?"

"Have you seen, Roman?" River asked, cutting his eyes around the classroom. He seemed unusually anxious as I approached the exit of the classroom, peeling open the door to show him the full view of just me.

"Roman left minutes ago. Why?" I voice causing River to keep shaking with nerves. I extend a hand to the shoulder of the blonde, squeezing it. "What's wrong?"

River leads me to the gym with pale skin, shocked while unsure of how to explain what was wrong. He gestured to the blood soaked gym of a massacre. He was like a fish from water,

CHAPTER THIRTEEN

proceeding to open then close his mouth. "A good portion of Bluebell Springs High School was just wiped out."

My eyes scan the sea of blood gushing students while Principal Waters is standing with her mouth agape. I couldn't believe she was the one frozen over in fear. I see Theodore with a deep wound, bleeding through his yellow and black plaid long sleeve. "River, there!"

Gavin had long climbed from the pile of unmoving students, crawling over to Theodore, scooping his head onto his lap. A scowl clung to his lips as blood stains were on his face with a splash of dirt. He was shaking like a leaf when River and I approached him. "Wh-Who did this to us?"

"Is he dying?" River whispered with tears, springing to life in his cornflower blue eyes. He saw the barely aware Gavin slowly nod his head in reply.

"He can't die. He's only fifteen." I hissed to River, crouching down beside him, meeting the void in the bright blue eyes of Gavin Mitchell. I could tell that if he lost his best friend that he would snap, probably blow up the rest of the world with no care.

"How do we save him, Gav?" River asks, still shaking as Gavin scowls, searching for an answer to our question.

Gavin places his hands over the wound of Theodore. A gold and lavender glow intermingle, making beautiful light as it seeps into his best friend. He has tears remaining, just in case his idea falls through. "I-I can't heal him."

"How about getting him to Sloan University?" I whisper in question to Gavin who vigorously nods his head. I'm going to take the leap with the blonde, not wanting to see the brother of my two friends die.

River cleared his throat. "I'm coming with you two. He's my

brother. I might have lost Roman in this bloody massacre. I can't possibly lose another brother."

Gavin let's River pick up Theodore, pressing into the chest of his brother. He's going to have to lead the way to a purple and pink stop sign around Bluebell Springs High School. He was good at spotting them even when he briefly showed me. "O-okay, let's go!"

As we walk, leaving the rest to either call the authorities or suffer; something does occur to me. I'd risk it once we got to Sloan University, not before. "Riv, I get that you're hysterical, but there is no way Roman is dead. I just saw him moments prior to you retrieving me from the empty classroom we were conversing in."

Gavin jogs over to a purple and pink stop sign, nodding for us to touch a hand to it. He was paving the way to save his best friend who was more than that to him. "This is how we get to Sloan University."

"Where could he have gone? He didn't return to the assembly, I don't think." River softly murmured, doing as Gavin did by touching a hand to the stop sign.

I was already ahead of River, having been gripping the stop sign. I didn't know where Roman would go, especially after the humiliation he seemed to face from Jesse and me. I sided with Jesse on his belief that no matter your sexuality, you wouldn't burn for that alone. I feel like other factors such as killing had to be involved unless it was self defense. "It was revealed that Five Seconds of Winter weren't all girls; he always drooled over Fievel Wong."

River snorted. "I could have told you that they weren't girls. Sure, they trick people with their animated videos, but have you ever listened closely to one of their songs? There is no way you miss their actual voices unless you need an excuse to hide something."

I lift an eyebrow, watching River become embarrassed for his middle brother. "I know your parents are strict."

"Roman and our dad were close for the longest of time until his first kiss at thirteen. I have never seen our father so off the rails beating Roman until he bled using his belt." River irritably mused, shaking his head at the dark memory.

Gavin raised an eyebrow, saying the name of the place while thinking deeply of Sloan University. He was able to get us right in front of the school just before one crosses the threshold of the pink colored building. He ushered us along as if Theodore couldn't wait which was a hard fact. "Is that why your mom isn't with him anymore?"

"Yes and no. There are other reasons that we can address later." River groaned, carrying his youngest brother into Sloan University. He was more amazed by the school than I had been when first setting foot onto the grounds.

"Amir should know what to do." Gavin said, heading straight for the office of the Headmaster. He attended Sloan University, so he would know where the office was.

I'm happy Gavin was leading the way, because I couldn't recall my way around. I vaguely remember my step-mother dropping me off, trying to exile me from my childhood house. I cut my eyes around, wondering if my sister would appear.

Amir Jones wasn't alone when we barged into his office. He was caught off guard, frowning since he had been in a deep discussion with the one person I hadn't expected to see again quite so soon. "Which is why…"

"Headmaster Jones!" Gavin shrieked, causing the man to trail off.

Amir squeezed the shoulders of Jesse whose icy blue eyes landed directly on me. He turned to face us. "What's with the shrillness…? Ah, Theodore Treanor!"

Gavin had silent teats, streaming down his cheeks as River carried Theodore closer to the Headmaster. "He was stabbed. There was a massacre at Bluebell Springs High."

I was choosing to avoid the officially concerned blue eyes of Jesse. My eyes were focused on those who currently commanded my attention. "Gav can't heal him."

"I see. I think I might know what could heal him. Follow me." Amir said, plucking up a set of giant, round, black and silver keys.

Jesse said nothing, clearing his throat. "Should I wait for you here?"

Amir cut his eyes from the keys to his younger, half brother than to me before he shook his head. "Jesse, you can follow us. I'm sure you'll want to since…"

As my cheeks burned red with the man trailing off, I pushed away the implications of what the Headmaster was attempting to get at. "Shouldn't we hurry or are we going to let Theo fade into the night?"

Amir led the way to a third, secluded set of stairs, close to being an attic but was a third landing of Sloan University. He sighed as we explored the stoned, doom and gloom, gothic corridor. He gestured for us to copy him once he entered a type of medical room. "Lay him on the bed."

Chapter Fourteen

Amir Jones tried everything he could in order to spare the life of Theodore Treanor. Hanging his head in defeat, he knew it was over when the fifteen year old refused to gasp for air. He was beyond a failure, aware that his time was coming to be hung out to fry. He begins to pace in front of the bed where Theodore lay, trying to conjure up new thoughts on how to save the boy. An idea came to mind. "Does anyone know if he has a special ability?"

Jesse cast his eyes to us, mostly looking at me. He cleared his throat. "A special ability could help to save his life. It would be easier to heal with some type of ability whether it's—"

"No, Theo doesn't have a special ability. Between Roman and I; he wasn't gifted or special." River took sharp breaths upon answering Jesse, interrupting the man.

Jesse tapped his fingers on his blue jeans, wondering how he could help. "I don't…"

Amir snapped his fingers to Jesse. "There may be a way. Couldn't you…?"

Jesse was already shaking his head in disregard to what Amir was attempting to suggest. He waved his hands in the air. "It's a bad idea to try that, he'll want to burn us; me specifically for your bad suggestion."

"He can't burn you." Amir said with hope evident in his bright blue eyes.

My candy apple green eyes had finally landed on the lean, lanky, porcelain complected male who made it hard to distance myself from. My contract may have been ripped up but Jesse had been telling the truth. Attraction had nothing to do with a piece of paper; all to do with feelings I had been sure didn't exist prior to the man. My tongue becomes tied before my eyebrows raise. "What can you do to save Theodore Treanor?"

Jesse folded his arms to his chest, lowering his icy blue gaze. He was wearing a gray, long sleeve shirt underneath his blue denim jacket that he had already stripped off. He must have taken said jacket off earlier as he gestured to Theodore. "I can do something that's considered illegal on behalf of daddy dearest, but should I risk it?"

"No one here can sway your decision, only you have the power to decide." I remark, catching his eyes as thoughtfulness plagued him. I see the man nod his head while contemplating the suggestion. I knew most people assumed you could influence a decision, but I don't agree.

"Would you leave the room? If there are any witnesses then they may burn just the same." Jesse spoke, blowing a breath. His eyes flickered from me once more to the floor, laced with shame over his oncoming betrayal.

I have this urge to say something to Jesse, but I have no idea what to say. I fidget with my fingers, slowly exiting the medical room; standing with River, Gavin and Amir. "I wonder if he's really going to help him or..."

"Don't think so negatively, Sae." River pipes up, not wanting anymore darkness in his head. He frowned before he sighed. "We need to find those who massacred Bluebell Springs High

CHAPTER FOURTEEN

or most of them. I didn't see any pink dust this time, but what do you want to bet that it's the same person?"

"Like a copycat?" Gavin quipped while Amir chose to process the newfound theory. He still had blood staining his cheeks, not that he cared given what happened to Theodore. "It's plausible."

"Do you have any proof that it's a copycat?" Amir asked a good question. His eyes jumped from each of us as I sighed.

"No, but I'm no murderer. As many times as I have deeply dreamed of being the next Dexter Morgan; female edition—there's no actual way I could kill a man." I half tease, watching River become livid once more.

River wiped the sweat from his palms down on the front of his navy green knit sweater. "I should go back to the crime scene. If I do, I may be able to see who did this or get a closer glimpse into it."

"What if this wasn't done by a person?" Amir challenged, beginning to disagree with River returning to the crime scene at Bluebell Springs. He couldn't stop the eighteen year old even nor could he stop Gavin and me. He was chewing on the thought of what to do. "I'll keep your brother for as long as it takes for him to heal and recuperate, but don't do more damage."

"The damage is done, Headmaster Jones. I think I can take care of myself. Oversee, Gav and Sable." River scoffed, shaking his head before he gestured from Amir to us.

Amir blew a raspberry once River rushed off, storming down the stairs, slamming the door shut of the school as he went along. He rubbed his face. "I cannot believe this is happening. When was the first murder or tragedy that brought on this domino effect?"

"Drew Jessup was killed—father of my everlasting bully. Dark pink glowing dust was found at the crime scene, but I wasn't anywhere near it." I gingerly reply as Gavin remains shut off, keeping his bright blue eyes on the floor.

Gavin plopped into a chair by the door, wanting to be left alone in order to kill the traitors off in his head. "I…"

I remained standing while they sat, starting to pace in front of the door to the medical room. I wanted to join River on his quest for justice, needing to reunite with Roman who might be able to aid us in finding '**The Copycat**' killer. "River will need back up so I'm going to have—"

The door of the medical room creaked open, slaying my words mid-sentence. There was no hope in his icy blue eyes that briefly connected with mine. He placed one hand in his pocket as he lied straight to our faces. "Theodore just needs plenty of rest, no visitors and time."

"What?" Gavin asked in an exasperated whisper. His bright blue eyes peered up at Jesse from his spot on the chair. He wasn't about to move or leave Theodore alone.

Amir became ghastly pale upon the words scratching his brain. "Even with the Breath of Fire, you couldn't save him from death?"

Jesse peered over at me before slowly glancing away as if the confirmation following would be any lighter. He sighed. "I tried, but I couldn't save him. Theodore Treanor is dead, resting his soul in eternity for however long my father sees fit. That was the price of going against his wishes, a soul for a soul."

I heard those words loud and clear. I did not want my soul for Theodore's soul. "Full disclosure, Gav, his father is Hades—God of the Underworld and Undead. Have fun with that!"

"Sable!" Jesse hissed in a dash of anger as I chose to stalk off, fleeing Sloan University. He shouldn't have let Theodore die nor should my soul have been traded on behalf of another. He called after me, making no move to follow me since I was in no mood to deal with him. "You had no right!"

Scoffing to myself, I had every right to inform my friends of the truth. I even had the right to tell my family members and their family members so they were safe from the devil that Jesse Wick was. I wring out my hands, making a break for the naturalistic view beyond the walls of Sloan University. "What the cat nuggets, is wrong with the skies?"

The skies had been stripped of the bright blue, having become black as night with the moon overseeing where the sun was. Storm clouds of gray came into play as orange and brown leaves from a maple tree swirled about in an angry, violent manner. There was one person who could be that tormented at the moment.

My hair begins to whip my face, as violent as the evil in the skies. The time of day should have shown the beautiful sun with cold winter grays. I won't head back into Sloan University so Jesse can yell or argue. It's what he obviously desires to which I refuse to give the man the satisfaction of. I end up at the stop sign, gripping it, thinking of River. I'm relieved when the bright blue skies come back at my next destination.

River Treanor is scowling at the sea of bloodied bodies with no help having been called. He gripped his curls, finally noticing how Principal Waters was frozen at the podium with her mouth agape. "This is all my fault!"

Hurrying towards the screech of River, I roll my candy apple green eyes. What took place wasn't his fault or anyone's fault. I extend a hand to his shoulder, feeling the blonde squirm with disturbance via the action. "How is this your fault? You were unaware like the rest of us!"

"If I had come clean about being a seer sooner, I would have been attending Sloan University, developing my ability. I would have been able to save them from this!" River roared, gatekeeping all the blame.

I'm about to correct River when the gleam of a familiar wheelchair catches my attention. I massage the temples of my forehead. Had my best friend gotten caught in the murder spree of **The Copycat**? I shove his shoulder. "Is-is that Erica?"

River snapped his head up, hearing faint coughing as his cornflower blue eyes followed mine to the wheelchair. His heart hammered in his chest as he got up, angrily throwing rubble and debris from the person bound to said wheelchair. He analyzed the blonde girl, checking her pulse, searching for any major damage. "It is Erica; she seems okay."

"Frightened, I take it." I softly mutter, striding closer to the pair. I saw a few light scratches but that was to be expected unless you got hit harder. My hands rest on my waistline as Erica is shaken up, scared, but not to the point of being mute. "Erica, did you see anyone perchance or anything that stood out to you?"

"Soft pink and brown leather." Erica informs us, still shaking like a leaf. She seems okay, now, that we had found her but it felt like someone was lingering.

River seemed less spooked since knowing somebody had survived. He took a deep breath. "I'm going to see if I can get a vision."

I bite my tongue to keep myself from informing him about the death of Theodore.

He wouldn't need that while trying to find who slayed half the students. He shakily crouched down, brushing his fingertips over some of the bloody students, rubble and debris, all the while, concentrating. He couldn't see much, mostly picking up on a ton of anger in pink and brown leather. A groan escaped his soft pink lips before he sighed. "I'm picking up on a ton of aggression with no clear image."

"It has to be a teenage girl." I half laugh, but I'm mostly serious when River snorts.

"Why would you be so narrow minded in this situation?" River asks, causing me to roll my eyes.

"Women, girls, etc. tend to be more aggressive in action, romance, you name it. We feel and experience our emotions more than men. I also don't see a teenage boy roaming around in leather with colors such as pink and brown unless you count Bow…" I close my mouth, trailing off. I didn't need to bring up one of my favorite Saturday Night Live comedians. "All in all, River, would you just trust me on this?"

Erica nods. "I agree with Sable on this. We do tend to have more rage than the average, jealous teen boy."

River harshly gulped, becoming truly scared of the opposite sex for a change. He cleared his throat. "Where do you suppose we take this investigation…of sorts?"

Chapter Fifteen

Pressing himself into the wall, River led the way to The Cozy Tavern. He agreed that we should go seek out Fievel Wong, Murphy Thrasher, and Tara Jessup. If his brother was snooping anywhere to garner information, The Cozy Tavern would be the place. He also knew how Roman enjoyed fighting while running his gator. Upon our arrival at the popular joint, River wanted us to blend in which was hard to do when it was overflowing.

"I'm just glad we didn't spring a ride from the purple and pink bus stop." I half groan, gaining a look to silence me from River. I shrug, thinking about Murphy who I thought I killed but he more than likely had an ability; of sorts. My mind vaguely recalled what Jesse Wick said, as if he knew the blonde was still alive which he probably did know. I hold up a hand to list off what could go wrong, but end up ranting about nothing we didn't already know. "The Cozy Tavern is a popular joint for those who deem themselves privileged above the rest of society!"

"Sable, can you not pick this moment to choose to be a drama queen?" River asks with the urge to place a hand over my mouth. His warning glare says it all as I take a few deep breaths.

My eyes scan the sea of familiar, overly popular kids to find

CHAPTER FIFTEEN

Roman standing off to the side with balled up fists. I could tell by his body language that things were about to go down badly. "I found your terse, livid brother."

Following my eyes to Roman, River sighs relief that Roman hadn't gotten injured or killed. His relief did remind me of how we lost Theodore causing me to continue to keep my mouth clamped shut. "What is he doing? He should have waited for us to get answers together!"

I internally agree, pursing my lips. I know we could have gotten answers together, but Roman was not a patient person. I shake my head. "Roman is as Roman does. He is stubborn, impatient and hot-headed. He would not have waited for us."

River's cornflower blue eyes flicked to my candy apple green eyes. Annoyance was present in his soulful, pretty gaze. "Do you really think so, Sae?"

I snorted, shaking my head of maple brown curls at River. I gently squeeze his shoulders. "River, be logical when it comes to the dodo brain for brothers you have."

"Come on." River sharply hissed to me before eagerly approaching Roman.

I had nothing to lose, walking with River to meet Roman who was glaring daggers into mostly Fievel Wong like the twenty three year old was the problem. Clearing my throat to gather the attention of Fievel and Murphy seemed to work. "Ladies."

Murphy chewed on his own tongue. He rolled his cobalt blue eyes. "Another crazed fan of Five Seconds of Winter, yeah? Let me clear the air for you, Sable; we did not trick our fans into believing we were girls or age appropriate. What you weirdos believe is on you."

Roman is working his jawline so hard into the ground, I believe he's about to let loose. "She's not a crazy fan of garbage people, who absolutely trick their fans."

Chuckling, Fievel Wong cast his honey brown eyes upwards to flit from me to Roman. His hair was caramel brown, parted to keep his bangs from blinding him. He was in a dark purple denim jacket with light blue denim jeans that maintained rips in either side of the knee. "You are kawaii."

"You are also adorable, sir, but we don't have time for games." I roll my green eyes, catching a blush growing on the cheeks of Roman.

Roman works his jawline some more, hum drumming on an uncertain idea of his. He snapped his fingers. "We need a more private area for these two half scums."

I would have asked Roman what he meant while a squeak escaped the soft pink lips of River. "Thought Projection?"

Roman moved us into a green room of sorts with no escape. He kept Fievel and Murphy planted in their chairs, allowing him to caress his chin in contemplation. "Where were you on the night of the murder of Andrew Jessup?"

Fievel frowned, letting his soft pink lips fall as his arms chilled. He folded his muscled, lean arms to his chest as he recalled the night. He would rather not have a repeat of that heartbreaking evening. "If I told you, I'd have to kill you."

There was a playfulness in his tone that matched sadness. My eyes scan him from head to toe while River scoffs. "It's just the five of us, Fiev."

"Good news is I have witnesses who can attest to where I was. My ex was at the gym, that's the day she broke up with me." Fievel solemnly spoke, shivering from the cold reminder.

River knelt down in front of the mixed boy. He extended a hand to the knee of Fievel who was scowling, aware that we would need to prove his innocence. "Thank you for your help,

CHAPTER FIFTEEN

Fiev. We know you're probably busy."

"I will go ahead and put it out there; whoever killed Drew set me up. They even decided to blow up Bluebell Springs High School which was more of a recent, isolated incident." I gingerly muse as false concern surfaced in the blue eyes of Murphy.

Murphy didn't once strike me the right way. He sat forward, becoming ever thoughtful. "You mean…?"

"Cut the act, Thrasher!" Roman snaps, shutting the blonde man up. His glare is heated beyond words as Murphy furrows his eyebrows. "You aren't good at acting."

River shook off the pain of the images that he saw from Fievel with his ex-girlfriend calling him all sorts of things under the sun. He felt bad for the man causing him to immediately twist his attention to the likes of Murphy. He quickly extended an arm to Murphy, picking up on the raging anger the man had. "It's the same type of anger belonging to the person who blew up Bluebell Springs High."

"My anger proves nothing." Murphy irritably notes, slinking back in the armchair, not too worried about anything. He folds his arms to his chest, keeping up the false charade of innocence.

"Murphy was at Bluebell Springs High, but did he blow up the school?" River has this glint of complication written across his fair features. He places a hand to his forehead, unsure of how to tell if Murphy was a danger to us.

"I wouldn't blow up your school. I was visiting in order to talk sense into Lila Darling. She's the only one who can keep my head level, but she's been missing from Bluebell Springs High for a good bit." Murphy groaned, yawning in the process causing me to snort. He must have been unaware of her graduation two years prior while unaware of her attendance at

Sloan University.

"My sister wasn't seeing the likes of you. In fact, she's getting married to a complete stranger." I lightly chuckle as Murphy becomes discomforted by the news.

"A stranger to you, but Simon Blackthorn has been my best friend for years. He's also besties with your man so I wouldn't take too much pride in your happiness for my dull, love life." Murphy mused, causing a bit of worry to seep into me.

"We don't have time for your games, Murphy. I get you probably care about no one in this world, but we do. We have to put a stop to whoever is doing this, because the next time; it'll more than likely be the entirety of Bluebell Springs." River groaned, cutting his eyes to Roman after they briefly stopped on me.

"I think you should try The Blue Court where they have all the files on our small town. I suggest as much since you may stumble across a few facts to help you." Fievel spoke up, wanting to help save his home town. He didn't fancy the idea of seeing Bluebell Springs destroyed by some maniac who lacked morals.

Murphy worked his jawline, cutting his cobalt blue eyes to me. He then cut them back to Fievel before gently nodding. "Fievel and I will tag along. What if you need backup?"

River and Roman exchanged a glance as if to decline the offer.

I noticed how Murphy kept cutting his eyes to me which made me wonder if there was more to the story, especially since he had been tying my sister's name into all of this. I cleared my throat. "Sure, we could use the extra help. If you try anything funny, you'll become castrated."

"I'm so scared." Murphy rolled his blue eyes before pushing himself to stand up. He recalled how we were elsewhere in private causing him to snort. "Do you mind returning us to

The Cozy Tavern? I'm going to have to use the bathroom before we head to The Blue Court where every file is documented."

Roman nodded his head causing the privacy of the green room to dwindle into nothing, like the snap of his fingers yet he didn't have to wave them in the air. He just dissolved whatever wall kept us from the real world. He sighed, taking the place of Murphy trying to unwind yet he was unable to. "Who's idea was it to have animated girls as your band?"

Fievel chuckled, cutting his honey brown eyes to the likes of Murphy. He knew the blonde was probably about to cut out on them. He knew how his friend got whenever trouble brewed on their doorstep. "It was definitely Murphy's idea."

"No one had to go along with him tricking people. Speaking of, where are the other two band members?" Roman inquired, searching the honey brown eyes of an amused, smirking Fievel. He scowled at the look, wanting answers as Fievel chuckled aloud.

"The other two members have been dead for years which is part of the reason we don't make new music. The other part is the fact that our label had us ghost singing for them." Fievel softly mused, becoming partly teary eyed at the painful reminder.

"How did they die?" River was curious upon asking, causing Roman to hit his brother in the abdomen. He shrugged. "I'm not trying to embarrass you, Roman or harass Fiev. I'm simply curious."

"Agreed." I reply just as the bathroom door is peeled open with a noisy Murphy returning to us. I see this glimmer of cold with a hint of dead seriousness in the blonde who met the eyes of Fievel. "What?"

"Kelly and May died in a bus crash. They were your age, like little sisters to us." Murphy reveals with a frown clinging to his full, pink lips. He could have been the guy you would leave your current partner for, if he wasn't so cold and off putting. He sighed. "Are we ready to go?"

"Like sisters to us?" Fievel scoffed, shaking his head in disagreement as he jabbed a finger in Murphy's chest. "You were having an affair with May."

"Excuse you, Fiev? They were the same age as Sable and Roman. I was not having an affair with them. Now, their older sisters, yeah." Murphy irritably corrected his friend. He remembered when the two girls tried to accuse him of false things when really it was their abusive, boyfriends at the time. "Do you not remember Terry and Garrett?"

"A little too well." Fievel harshly gulped, ungluing himself from the chair next to Roman. He gestured for us to follow him and Murphy. "We will take you to The Blue Court."

"I'm sorry about your loss." River mumbled, unsure of what to believe coming from Fievel and Murphy. He didn't like hearing mixed or twisted stories that just didn't make sense. He walked beside Roman, leaving me to makeup the back.

"Don't be sorry. Kelly and May had it coming. They were good singers, writers and musicians, but they were terrible people-ists." Murphy said, once more shrugging off any type of emotion for their dead band members. After what Fievel tried to accuse him of, he wouldn't be surprised if his friend suddenly went missing.

Chapter Sixteen

The Blue Court was made up a few stories, cemented in crystal, foamy green, sleek marble that made one want to stop and ogle the oval shaped building. It was where all the hearings, law breakers, and pretty much anything relating to the law took place. Citizens of the small town could elope as something nagged at the back of my brain. This version of the building was far off, way back with no other people coming or going. No vehicles were parked nor were any security guards present, truly stirring the concern within.

"Are you sure this is the right building?" I ask Murphy and Fievel as the two exchange a glance.

"In all honesty, this is the old court." Murphy informed me, nonchalantly shrugging. "You wouldn't find anything to help you, if we went to the current court—think about it."

"He's got a point." Fievel smoothly replies, gesturing to the outside. An eyebrow rose at the semi blue pine needles of the pine forest, surrounding the oval shaped building. "This one would have more records, leading you to a potential suspect."

"You mean this court has every record of every person born in Bluebell Springs and who has lived their entire lives in Bluebell Springs." River corrects, rolling his cornflower blue eyes. He sees Fievel crack a half smile before Murphy groans.

"Fiev and I will wait here for you losers to find what you're looking for." Murphy speaks up, clearing his throat as he makes a hand gesture to his good friend. His cobalt blue eyes held a secret of darkness that could betray us all.

"In that case, I will wait here with you losers in order to keep an eye on you. I don't trust you." Roman bitterly remarks to Murphy, correcting the twenty year old. He didn't find it right that they should want to appeal to those of us who weren't closer in their age nor could he be blamed.

"I could care less about who you trust versus who you don't trust." Murphy irritably announces, folding his arms to his chest. He becomes guard-like as I enter The Blue Court with River.

"Do you suppose they could be telling the truth?" I gently inquired, causing River to snort.

"Murphy is overloaded with anger. Fievel is the only one of the two being remotely honest. Who is Murphy protecting?" River muttered, walking as close to me as he possibly could. He was the vanilla to my spice.

I nonchalantly shrug my shoulders. Couldn't I force Murphy to tell me using my ability of manipulation? I still didn't even know what the deal was with whatever I had. I stop River at the landing of the stairs we chose to take, upwards. "Shouldn't we try the files in the basement?"

"If I remember correctly which it's possible that I don't, Sable then the files in this particular court are in the attic." River informs me as my fingers brushed the navy green railings of the stairs. He leads the way in silence as dust clouds our lungs. "That door…"

I was already striding to the door he mentioned, shoving it open, only to faceplant until cracked, creaking floorboards.

CHAPTER SIXTEEN

Half a hole was in the floorboard, almost making me become one with the downstairs of the old Blue Court. "Shoot."

"Sae, are you okay?" River asks as he extends his hands to help pull me to my feet. He frowns when his eyes scan the attic. "How can this be so messed up? It makes it nearly impossible to get to the files."

"We can walk on the beams for support. Only half of the floorboards are ripped up." I groan, tired of the day. I attempt to walk on the beams for support, clinging to the wall because my plan instantly backfires.

"Would you two like some assistance?" The amused, monotone voice of Jesse Wick pipes up from the doorway. His arms are folded over the gray long sleeve he's wearing. His black hair remained parted, becoming messy in action. His icy blue eyes show no concern causing me to scoff. "I could fix your floorboards, but I'm owed an apology."

River scowled in my direction. "What did you do to upset him?"

"I'll figure it out. We don't need his help, just because he's a melodramatic drama queen." I kindly inform River, shrugging off any form of help from Jesse. I already had my back turned to the man, planning to keep it that way.

"Don't be stubborn, Sable. You could use my help." Jesse said, letting up on some of his own stubbornness. If one didn't know any better, he could almost match me, but he wasn't needed in my book or anywhere else.

"I won't ask for your help. I won't beg. You have me pegged as a fool. I'd rather work out my issues so hard, it kills me versus asking somebody for anything." I gently muse, keeping steady as I cling to the beams. I wonder if I could use my ability to manipulate the files, into coming our way.

River had been in contemplation mode, stroking his chin as his cornflower blue eyes held wonderment. "Sae, how about you try to manipulate the files into flying our way?"

"You could try. It may work." Jesse agreed with the drawl in his voice ever-present. He wasn't from the south nor was his drawl southern; it was just his tone of voice which made him seem weird to those with a normal tone. "I didn't mean to overdo the jealousy or anger, Sable. I'm sorry."

Ignoring the pale skinned, blue eyed jerk, I keep focus on the task at hand. Forcing myself to will the files in our direction. As they are engulfed in a dark pink glow with a shower of glitter, said files come zooming at us, so hard that they knock the breath from Jesse; slamming into the man. I hear a groan, thud, and an exasperated gasp. "Okay, before you growl at me, that was a legitimate accident, Jess."

"No worries." Jesse grumbles while River crouches down, hovering above him. He hands River a file or two, leafing through others in his lap. A frown clings to his lips, unsure of what we're searching for. "What exactly are we meant to be looking for, Sae?"

I hurry back over to them, gaining an angry scratch from a piece of the floorboard on my lower leg. I briefly wince, snatching a file from his hand with his eyes on me. "We are looking for someone who has the copycat gene, Jess."

Jesse scoffed. "There was only ever one person's family with that gene. They were exiled, slaughtered so order was kept in Bluebell Springs. Why didn't you start with that earlier? You could have avoided wasting time."

"We realized after I wound up at the crime scene before Sable came to retrieve me so we could embark on uncovering what has been taking place. We put two and two together at the

CHAPTER SIXTEEN

school, discovering Principal Waters had indeed been killed. We were unsure before we brought Theodore to you." River decided to inform Jesse, going with a long winded explanation.

"Don't ask how Theodore is either. We finally stumbled across something to revive him." The words mindlessly, wordlessly fell from the lips of Jesse. He hadn't been aware that River didn't know about the brief death of Theodore Treanor. "As I was saying—"

River dug his fingers into his short, golden blonde hair. His eyes held a gleam of danger as they set on me. "Theodore died? When were you going to tell me?"

"When this was over. Theodore, having died, wouldn't have spared anyone of what's to come thanks to the copycat." I half snapped at River, making sure the blonde couldn't come back at me.

Jesse extended a hand to keep me from lunging at River. He shook his head. "If you two want to argue about that factor later then be my guest. As is, we have to focus on the events at play."

"What's in the copycat gene? Why is it called that?" River chose to do as Jesse suggested, choosing to ignore me. He was good at a lot of things, but acting wasn't one of them. His eyes remained on Jesse who was inhaling sharply.

"It's in the name, River. The copycat gene holds properties of an ability to copy, mirror, mimic and steal. They don't necessarily go hand in hand, but this gene can ruin plenty of lives." Jesse voices with sadness in his eyes.

My heart flutters a few times. I process the information, sitting back on my hindlegs. I'm about to ask a question I know I'm going to regret. "Who in Bluebell Springs has this gene? Who present could be doing this?"

"The issue with the copycat is the fact that it's a genetic disorder that distorts the mind. The person with it can be kind, good natured, most especially in their intentions, but they snap and kill when too much stress is put on the brain." Jesse proceeded to explain, terrified to reveal the name. "Doesn't matter if it's stress about nothing, it can make the person with the gene go insane."

I grow suspicious of Jesse, watching him snort via my reaction. I open my mouth then close it; I've long since leaned in closer to the man. "Are you admitting to being the Copycat?"

"Are you insane, Sable?" Jesse quizzed, darkly chuckling before shaking his head. He sighed. "No, but those with this gene did come into contact with my ancestors. Lovers on lovers, hardly married."

"Give us a name!" River hissed, ready to pop Jesse a couple of times. He refrained from hitting Jesse, yearning for a reason as Jesse winced.

Jesse briefly looked at River only to glance at me. He extended a hand softly to my cheek, causing warmth to spread between us. He then lowered his hand as sadness engulfed him. "Have you heard of the name, Timothy Bluebell?"

My eyes landed on the floor beneath the man as I played a game of connect the dots. I did know of the name causing my olive complexion to become pale. Inhaling sharply, I shake my head of thick, maple brown curls. "Are you telling me that I have an ancestor with the Copycat gene?"

River is brushing his fingers under his chin as he scoffs. He snaps his fingers, causing me to look his way. "Isn't Lacey's father, Timothy Bluebell Junior?"

"If you are going to start accusing Lacey of being some psychopath with a vengeance to kill, I will disown our friendship."

CHAPTER SIXTEEN

I quickly snapped at the blonde boy who sighed.

"I'm not trying to accuse her. What if her father is still doing bad things on behalf of his ancestors?" River posed the question, shaping things into order for me.

I raise an eyebrow at the blonde, having torn my eyes away from Jesse. "How are we going to catch him in the act if it is him?"

Jesse stretched his long, slender limbs into the air. He yawned as he chose to ask the hard question. "Why do you want to rule Lacey out? Is it because you two share DNA? What if she is the one doing this?"

"I can't..." I trail off but Jesse scoffs, pulling himself to his feet.

Jesse brushes dust off of his jeans. "It's family in your eyes. Why would you fancy asking the difficult questions? I'm heading back to Sloan University. You two are welcome to join, but leave behind Fievel and Murphy. They aren't needed in figuring this out. Amir should know what to do."

I allow his words to register in my brain, following after the man. I hear River shout for Roman, telling him that we needed him. I didn't want to believe it could be Lacey Pringle—the cousin I had known since childhood. I know she was having mood swings as of late, but that didn't mean anything. I wouldn't chalk it up to the Copycat gene. "You better not just be blowing smoke, Jess."

Jesse sighed. "I'm not just blowing smoke, Sae. I don't want to be right. I have family too, so I get how the idea of betrayal from blood would sting."

"Did your father betray you? Is that how you know?" I ask Jesse who stays silent, giving me an answer within itself. I tense once River comes jogging towards us with Roman following his lead. I assume Jesse opened a portal, because it's only when the Treanor brothers appear that I realize we were standing front and center at the heart of Sloan University.

Jesse kept walking, believing we were going to get down to the bottom of whatever was happening in one day.

Chapter Seventeen

FIVE MONTHS LATER...

The Copycat went silent after slaying Drew Jessup and blowing up a bunch of Bluebell Springs High School students. In doing so, said person wasn't caught even with the discovery of the connection to Timothy Bluebell. No proof meant no one could do anything about it aside from a crap ton of research. Turning nineteen on the twenty seventh of March—present in the Spring of April, didn't make me thrilled about the rebirth. Blowing a raspberry, a familiar voice that had long disappeared startled me from my morbid thoughts.

"There my Sae is." Jesse Wick jokes, coming into view. He was in all black, walking like he could take whatever he wanted with no care in the world. His arms were folded to his chest, proving how guarded the man was. "Heard anything since attending Sloan University? I'm happy you caved, but was it worth it?"

I had gotten a much better grip on my ability, able to control it at will. I didn't need his help or anyone else. I switched to Sloan University after the Bluebell Springs High incident, accompanied by River and Roman. "It was worth it, to finally find my place and allow myself to feel as if I belong somewhere in the world."

Biting his bottom lip, Jesse kept a distance from me. He

seemed doubtful, reproachful of coming closer. "I'm going to stay over here."

"Ah, I'm assuming for the crap that you've been getting on behalf of what you can't control." I muse, thinking of the twisted, backwards world we live in. You could be nineteen and know what you want with the rest of the world disagreeing. Who needs the approval of unhappy strangers? "How about I come to you?"

"No, Sae, just stay put. I didn't come to distract you from your life." Jesse said, shaking his head. He seemed rather uncomfortable, making me uncomfortable and uneasy. Why did he choose to pull back suddenly, when prior he was all about invading my personal space? He had been off doing whatever for five months straight, leading me to wonder about his desire before.

"I'm not sure, the Copycat is even still alive. It was reported that Timothy Bluebell Jr. died. I'm thinking this means that it was in fact him." I eagerly muse with Jesse taking the information into consideration.

Jesse slowly began to nod his head, tensing when an ear splitting scream filled the atmosphere. He frowned, rushing to move once the lights of Sloan University began to flicker like we held a ghostly presence. He pressed into me while overlooking the railing of the school stairs. "Is that Erica Mitchell?"

Erica Mitchell was bound to her wheelchair, gagged, hanging from the chandelier of strawberry crystals dangling over the sea of students. Her eyes were rolled to the back of her eyes. She was dead with no way of saving her.

Roman had come rushing from his dorm with a half naked Fievel following while trying to gather himself. He parted his lips. "Not Erica! I was going to marry River to her!"

CHAPTER SEVENTEEN

Fievel lightly hovered over Roman, shaking his head as tears began to prick the back of his eyelids. "Oh gosh! She was so innocent."

River gasped, being the last to come into view of the landing on the second floor. He hurried down the stairs, staring up at Erica, angrily pulling at his short, blonde hair. "How do we get her down?"

We were all pretty much panicking as Jesse vanished into darkness that swarmed the corpse of Erica, removing the poor girl from the ceiling.

"Who could have done something like this?" River sobbed, clinging to Erica once Jesse set her on the ground, becoming a clear image of an emotionless person. Fresh tears kept coming from him as loud cackling boomed overhead, shaking the school.

"I could have done something like this!" A familiar, feminine voice growled at us. She had a hard on for rage, murder and the occult. She wasn't just anyone, proving me wrong in my belief that my cousin couldn't be this far gone.

"Lace?" River croaked, having believed the writer was a decent person. He fell for her tricks too, like we all did.

Jesse hovered over River and Erica, turning his gaze of icy blue to me. He was attempting to come up with a game plan to protect us all. "What do you want, Lacey?"

Laughing like a maniac, she found her voice. "Lacey? Good one."

My memory came to serve me correctly causing a plan to form in my head. I tore my eyes from Jesse, River and Erica, stepping away from their view. I cut my eyes to the right in the direction of the dorm that belonged to my cousin. I caught the curiosity within Roman and Fievel who had been involved over the past few months. I shake my head at them, gesturing for them to stay where they're at.

I recall how I walked in on Roman and Fievel experimenting with one another, moaning and scarring me for life. My father had come back around, signing the deed over to me and Lila who had simply eloped with Simon. My father insisted on a family dinner with Aelita Treanor and her sons in order to celebrate life and how good it could be. What about how bad it could be for those less fortunate? I asked about Lacey only for my father to wave her off of any family inheritance.

My father mentioned something about her family stemming from the devil himself, how she wouldn't suffer in place of us. I was heartbroken by how off putting and cold the man could be, but afterwards he fled with Maria. I caught Roman and Fievel together that dinnertime, yearning to scrub the intricate picture from my brain. I could understand if they were planning to spend the rest of their summers together…

"Ahem." Roman cleared his throat, regaining my attention.

I silently slink off towards the direction of Lacey's dorm which had her name written on a silver and pink plaque. I forgot how infatuated with pink and brown leather she had been in the past. If I had recalled that sooner then we would have been alright—all of Bluebell Springs.

Flinging open the dorm door, she's standing there in the middle of the room, but it's not Lacey Pringle. It's the one person shunned from the family, who we aren't allowed to speak or think about. She was dressed in a black tutu with a black tank top, chalky skin with black makeup. No, she's not trying to be goth or emo, believing her personality to be one with her true love; Sin Bluebell. "I am going to make you all pay."

CHAPTER SEVENTEEN

Creating a workable, clean, cool butcher knife from mid-air using my dark pink manipulation; I plunge the knife deep into her spine, severing the cord. I hear Darcy Bluebell grunt, groaning before her lifeless corpse drops to the ground. All in all, it was easy for me to forget she existed in our family tree since she changed her last name from Pringle to Bluebell. I always found it eerily spooky how she was the identical twin of Lacey Pringle until Darcy tried to change her appearance; twisting until her almond brown hair was the only thing to associate the similarities between the twins. I hear the thud of Darcy's chalky body drop but my candy apple green eyes are narrowed on Lacey.

Lacey Pringle is duct taped to a chair with a sock stuffed in her mouth. There's duct tape keeping the sock in place as silent, but fresh tears slip from her brown eyes. She's beyond terrified, shaking like a leaf. She's shaking her head as we watch the reddish pink ability leave Darcy only to enter her. "H-Halph, may!"

I rush over once my weapon dissolves, feverishly untying the teary eyed, shaking Lacey. I quirk any eyebrow. "Did you just absorb the copycat gene slash ability?"

"Sae, I've always had the gene. It's an ability that I do not want. Can you manipulate it from my body? I don't want to wake up one day, doing what Darcy did." Lacey sobbed, burying her face into the crook of my shoulder; making it wet.

Disgust surfaces on my olive features as I pat her back, rubbing soothing circles into it. I don't like certain liquids or things to touch me unexpectedly. Her tears splashing my shoulders was highly unexpected. "I can try to manipulate the copycat ability from you, Lace. I don't know how good it'll do."

"Don't bother. The ability needs a living host or it'll inject society with worse things than what Darcy was giving in place of her twin." Jesse came into view, analyzing Lacey. He nodded to her. "You need the medical room in which we will call it the Infirmary like a normal school. Amir is crazy."

"I d-don't want this." Lacey stuttered as a fresh set of tears came strolling down her cheeks. She had this plea in her voice, making me wonder if I couldn't manipulate her into accepting the ability until there was a way around it.

"You may want to fight this, but you can't." Jesse stated, matter-of-factly. He walked past me, placing one of Lacey's arms around his shoulder. He briefly cut his eyes to me before clearing his throat. "We should talk once things calm down."

"We definitely should." I agreed, mostly needing some time to collect my own thoughts. I would have helped Jesse get Lacey to our newly agreed upon infirmary, but what would be the point? I'm sure Lacey would need some time to understand everything that had taken place. Switching from Bluebell Springs High to Sloan University had proved breathable, setting my heart at ease when peace had been real over the past five months.

I exit the dorm of Lacey Pringle, wondering who would clean up the dead bodies at Sloan University. I should probably ask Amir who would more than likely be in his office. I stopped to check on Roman and Fievel who were eyeing River cradling Erica.

"Where's my sister?" Gavin Mitchell burst into the room, having been unaware of what happened until minutes ago. He tugged at his curls with his boyfriend striding into view, gifting him with soothing circles. He was just as broken up about Erica's murder as equally as River appeared to be.

I couldn't leave River hanging, causing me to act, taking the steps two at a time to reach him. I had been present when

CHAPTER SEVENTEEN

Theodore finally asked Gavin to be his boyfriend, sharing their first kiss in the kitchen of Aelita Treanor. They were meant to be cooking dinner but things sparked to life within seconds of their feverish kiss. I place my chin on the crook of River's neck, holding the blonde for a change as something awakens within. "Riv, it'll be okay."

River turned his face into my chest, disagreeing with my sentiment. He had just turned nineteen a week ago, losing Erica wasn't on his card let alone anyone's card. "I have bad luck! Erica and I were becoming closer as friends, talking about everything from our love of nature to our crushes."

I kept River safe in my arms, unsure of what else to do. All I could do was comfort the blonde who cried it out until his face pressed into my neck. "I am so sorry, River."

Amir Jones cleared his throat to capture our attention. Having snapped his fingers, he cleared Sloan University of the corpses that were Erica and Darcy. "We will reset the mind, clearing it of all the morbid parts. Welcome to the restart of Sloan University!"

Deja vu shook my soul as the feeling of nothingness washed over me. I was reminded of the beginning of Bluebell Springs High in early September. I remove myself from River who doesn't fight it, looking and seeming just as emotionless as me. My eyes dart around connecting to the icy blue of Jesse Wick who is sporting a deep frown.

"Sae, what just happened?" River whispered to me in a hoarse voice. "I'm not sad or bitter about her murder and I should be!"

I extend a hand doused in sweat to his shoulder. "How about you stay put? I'll ask someone who knows."

Jesse whispered something to Amir who both glanced in my direction. "Sable Darling, shouldn't you be in class?"

I shake my head at Jesse, parting my lips in disbelief. "You're the son of Hades. You made it a big deal that we were connected. What's changed?"

"Everything has changed, Sable. Everything." Jesse piped up, pressing his lips into a line. His eyes bore no emotion, no warmth prior to whatever Amir Jones did to us.

As shock flooded my veins, I couldn't help but wonder what other secrets were buried in Bluebell Springs, hiding in plain sight. I pout as I stalk off before choosing to plop down on the bottom of the stairs at Sloan University. How could Jesse Wick suddenly turn cold on me? The logic didn't make sense. I was going to get to the bottom of the new mystery even if it killed me.

Chapter Eighteen

Hot and silent tears were streaming down my cheeks. Lifting a hand in my sleep to wipe away the tears stirred alarm within. Since when did I start crying in my sleep? Panic shot through me causing me to bolt upright in my bed at Sloan University. The light automatically flicked on beside my bed, on the nightstand causing irritation to rise in me.

I couldn't stand the bright light. I placed a hand to my eyes to keep the light from making my head feel funny. Warm, gooey, and red were my tears as I pulled my fingers from my closed eyes. My eyes widened as the stench of blood hit me like a train ramming into an innocent bystander. I couldn't remember how I even got to Sloan University, but something deep down told me Jesse Wick and Headmaster Jones knew what happened to my memory.

Waking up in blood was not on my bingo card this year. My body was soaked in the disgusting stuff causing my nose to wrinkle. My heart is racing a hundred miles per minute in my chest. *What should I do? Who do I trust?*

Wringing out my hands in a panic, I force myself from the bed only to hear the clatter of metal meeting the floor. My eyes traveled down to the butcher knife that had been entrusted to me at some point during my blackout party. My vision began to cloud with dizziness while I began to back up so my back could press into the cool of the wall. How could I have killed somebody while I slept? I don't rapidly blink or nothing; keeping my eyes squeezed tightly shut in hopes I'll wake up from my new nightmarish reality.

"One, two, he's coming for you!" A voice erupted in the back of my head causing shivers of discomfort to run down my spine. The voice was that of a male, taunting me while my heart grew faint in my chest.

I would have asked who was speaking but sweat currently covered my body with disconnect buzzing in my eardrums.

"Sable!" River gently hissed, coming into view. His cornflower blue eyes burned with concern, sadness and anger. His short, fair blonde hair was disheveled; almost making the twenty year old look like a mad man. His touch actually kept me sane for the most part.

"R-River?" I stuttered while attempting to keep my voice in check as a scowl lit up my bright green eyes. I come down to Earth just as River explains to me what's happening.

"Somebody broke into Sloan University, wiped out the entire gifted beings of the school, and chose to frame…" River trailed off, casting his eyes around my dorm room. He dropped his hands from my shoulders, toying with the gnape of his neck. He's nervous now.

"Wiped out?" I squeak in a weak tone of voice while River is opting to inch a little bit away from me. My eyes widened even further as something clicked in my brain. "What about my sister, cousin, and your brothers?"

"Take a deep breath, Sable. I know you wouldn't kill them… on purpose." River gingerly informs me, causing a glare of daggers to shoot up from me.

CHAPTER EIGHTEEN

My hands rest on my blood soaked waistline. I need to get showered, changed, and ready to slay another monster. *Another monster?* My fuzzy memories were trying to surface as that same male voice from moments ago cackles in the back of my brain.

"You were set up by the devil incarnate, but the joke's on you. That's what you get for trusting him." The deep, throaty male voice snickered, finding my situation funny.

I bit my tongue instead of replying out loud. I disliked the way my friend was looking at me. I hadn't lost my flipping mind. "River, this was not my work! We all know this."

River tugged at his collar. "Do we know this isn't your work? You've been framed for murder before, sure…"

I can't listen to the blonde utter another word. I head to the bathroom of cleanliness, wash my hands then snatch up a pair of fresh and not so bloody clothes. *It might kill me to discover who was setting me up a second time for murder, but what did I have to lose?* I take a shower and make sure all the blood is gone from every nook, cranny, and crevice of my body. I dry off, tugging on a pink blazer over a light gray long sleeve shirt with a black mini skirt over black stockings.

I try not to smirk, aware of my decent enough looks. I tug on my black, ankle boots, careful to avoid the blood once I exit the bathroom of my dorm. I cut my green eyes to River who is beyond worried, having overtaken my role of too much panic. "Riv, come on. You and I are very much aware that I did not do this."

"I know you didn't kill Tara's father, but this—" River stressed upon gesturing to all the blood. He was right to be as stressed as he was since somebody evidently had a field day with slaying the entirety of the school.

I extend a hand to manipulate the blood into a disappearing act. I won't be held accountable for something I didn't do. I stroke my chin as something runs through my brain. "Did you see Erica?"

Biting on his bottom lip in a gentle manner, confusion surfaces in his blue eyes. River furrows his blonde eyebrows, bringing his eyes to meet me directly. "I thought she was dead. She was found hanging from the ceiling."

"I saw her walking around—footloose and fancy free with no care in the world earlier in the evening." I inform the blonde of my recollection. I even exchanged a few words with the blonde girl who had this knowing smirk and gleam splashed all across her face.

"I don't believe you. Sweet Erica was wheelchair bound." River scowled, shaking his head at me. He wasn't going to help me catch '**this killer**' as acid rose in my throat.

"Were you in love with her?" I inquire, narrowing my eyes on the blonde who begins to sweat with unease.

River pursed his pink lips. "I'm saying nothing." He doesn't mutter another word while I opt to slip out of the dorm.

I hate the sight that beholds me once they set on the blood stained carpets and walls. Piercing screams scratch my brain causing it to feel swollen with pressure. I get part way down the hall when pale blue eyes, belonging to a boy with a lean and lanky stature becomes visible—he seems able to cloak himself with invisibility.

His pale blue eyes were set to a tanned, smug face with full, dark pink lips and a head of short, dark brown curls. He was in blue jeans, a dark brown button up long sleeve with brown boots. He pushed himself from leaning on the wall using his body to do so while nodding to acknowledge me. "You need to

CHAPTER EIGHTEEN

be careful around these parts, Miss Sable Darling."

I freeze in my tracks, having already manipulated the rest of the blood from the floors of Sloan University. I needed to get outside in order to breathe in the fresh air. I cut my eyes to the five foot ten boy. It took me a minute to realize he had been the one speaking in my head moments ago. "Says who?"

"Oh, I'm Casper Wick." He extends a hand for me to shake but the smugness intertwined with the coldness in his eyes puts me off. His eyes were pretty and he was handsome for somebody who looked to be related to Jesse Wick—the son of Hades.

"Half brother of Jesse Wick?" I gently mutter as my memory is coming back into tact. My memories had been failing me as of late with the Headmaster and Jesse coming to mind. I recall them whispering together, squeezing their mouths right shut when they saw me inching closer. I walked with ease and silence. Their freakout made no sense to me.

"Your memory is surfacing. That's good. I have a bone to pick with that loser known as Jesse and so does Hades." Casper pipes up, removing his hands from the pockets of his blue jeans. He's in the process of following me as I make my way out of the school—in front of Sloan University on the pavements of the sidewalk.

"Hades? Jesse is the son of Hades." I irritably inform Casper who snorts.

"Hades is my older brother. Jesse is my nephew and a darned fool. Amir Jones also has to answer for his betrayal of our family and contracted agreement." Casper softly explains as he stops me in my tracks once more. He places a hand on either side of my shoulder, peering down into my eyes.

I can see it in his eyes. I know what's about to happen as I work my jaw. I shake my head at him. "Don't you dare! I have to be up here in order to catch who offed the entirety of Sloan University."

Casper softly chuckled. "It was Hades. He wanted me to get my hands dirty, but like I told him, I'm just the soul collector."

"I'm going to Hell?" I squeak as Casper squeezes my shoulder.

"No, Sable, you aren't going to Hell. It's this lovely place called the Underworld. You are going to make such a lovely, beautiful bride." Casper advised, softly smiling as if his words brought me any comfort.

"B-Bride?" I become hysterical whereas Casper tuts. My panic returns, causing me to be on the cusp of doing something stupid. I tug at my brown curls. "I will not marry some old, washed up, ruler with no morals!"

Casper sighed, pinching the bridge of his forehead as he took in my wording. He shook his head. "It's not Hades, you'll be wed to. I promise, Sweetheart."

I searched the pale blue eyes of Casper Wick after the way he said the nickname many weren't fond of. I almost found it cozy and endearing, but I didn't know him. I barely knew Jesse Wick. "No."

Casper once more sighed. He gently rubbed soothing circles into one of my shoulders. He was doing what he could to butter me up. "You will come to get to know me, my older brother and nephew. Amir is a traitor who will answer to Hades for the crimes he has committed. Everything will be fine. You'll see, Sweetheart."

I'm sweating profusely as a plan formulates in my mind. I step closer to Casper as I produce a blue glowing dagger, readying myself to bury it deep within Casper. I won't be leaving Bluebell Springs or this place that's been my home for however long. "I am so sorry."

CHAPTER EIGHTEEN

"Me too." Casper said, reading me just as I went to burrow the dagger into his chest. He became transparent, allowing the dagger to bury into an invisible chest, going right through him. A frown placated his lips once he heard the metal clatter to the ground behind him. He was disappointed as he tutted, meeting my eyes with fury.

"You have to understand—" I open my mouth to nervously explain when Casper cuts me off. My mouth was moving, but my voice had been silenced by Casper who had waved his hand in the air. I didn't blame him. I did just try to kill him, out of fear of a future blanketed in darkness.

Casper took a few deep breaths, searching my green eyes with his pale blue ones once I gave up and closed my mouth. No emotion swept into his gaze once the glint of betrayal had vanished from his face. He forcibly tugged me into him, snapping his fingers to create a ring of blinding, blue flames that lapped at us before taking us directly to his home. He clung to me, keeping his arms wrapped snugly around me like caging somebody would make a difference. He didn't let go of his hold on me until I kept squirming in his arms.

I was going to have to trust Casper Wick if I wanted to survive the Underworld. I harshly gulped, having to silently accept my ill fated reality. My eyes cut to Amir Jones who was on his knees, in front of the one and only Hades. I'm assuming the former Headmaster of Sloan University was more or less waiting to be put on trial for his crimes against the God of the Undead. I didn't relax until Casper wasn't touching me so I could comprehend the new reality of my situation.

"Amir is about to go on trial. You are so welcome to testify for the man. Hades knows he'll need it." Casper gently nudged my shoulder.

In time, we all had to accept things we didn't want to accept, didn't we? I continue to keep my mouth shut in order to drum up a plan that will work in my favor.

Hades clears his throat, coughing as he paces in front of Amir Jones. He's wearing a navy green, short sleeve tee shirt that is made of cotton to match black jeans. He's broad shouldered, olive complected with hazel brown eyes. His hair appears to be a short, light brown with this anger seeping from him. He shakes his head at Amir. "Time and time again, you let me down, Amir!"

Fiddling with my fingers, I had my emerald green eyes wandering to the roof of the Underworld which was layered under thick caves. A silent sigh came out in heaves as sadness swept me. *Would my family come for me? Would my best friends remember who I am? I* yearned to get home to Bluebell Springs, missing my hometown the longer I'm forced to remain in purgatory.

Amir whimpered before Hades did what he was known for— he killed Amir in cold blood with the touch of a blue flamed fingertip. Amir's body became a ghastly gray before he dropped with no life in him to the ground.

"Hades." Casper spoke the name of his older brother who frantically cast hazel brown eyes towards him. He slowly approached Hades unsure about the decision. "Are you alright, brother? We can come back."

Hades' attention turned to me. A crooked smile reached his dark pink, full lips as he began to rub his hands together. "Is this for me?"

I scoff, rolling my emerald green eyes. "I'm not for you or anyone. Return me to my home!"

Casper cut me a glare before waving me off like I was an

CHAPTER EIGHTEEN

invisible shadow that lingered. "No, that's Sable Darling."

Hades tilted his head, briefly forcing his eyes from me before they returned. He seemed to hold a renewed interest in me. "Sable Darling? Are you a child of...?"

"Possibly." Casper hissed, picking up where Hades trailed off. He didn't want me to overhear what they knew. His pale blue eyes held deep enthusiasm. "She doesn't know, we should probably keep it as such."

"What's going on?" I ask, extending my hands outwards. I might need to fight my way out of this messy situation I had gotten myself stuck in.

Casper pursed his lips, frowning before cutting his eyes to Hades. He lowered his pale blue eyes to the cave of the Underworld, deciding whether he should answer me or not.

Hades, on the other hand, didn't want me to know. His eyes were blazing with deep hatred and anger. His nostrils began to flare. "You are a child of two people that we do not speak of! Those people should have learned from their mistakes yet chose not to!"

"I know who my parents are. You're going to have to try again." I voice before releasing a yawn into the atmosphere.

Casper cleared his throat to gather my attention. He motioned for me to walk with him while leaving Hades alone to his thoughts and himself. He lightly pressed the palm of his hand to the small of my back. "He's going through some stuff."

"Are you going to tell me the truth?" I ask Casper who has this smirk written in his pale blue eyes.

Casper nods, but stops me short. He pulls me into him, cupping my face only to press his lips feverishly to mine. Soft, delicate and nurturing. "With time, the truth will come to be yours, Sweetheart."

About the Author

Madaline Geneva Clifton is a feverish writer who stops at nothing to ensure her voice will be heard. She loves crafting fictional worlds with fictional characters and settings. Her favorite genre to dabble in is fantasy with a blend while being open to writing other genres. She loves nature, music, animals, and being able to breathe in fresh air.

Milton Keynes UK
Ingram Content Group UK Ltd.
UKHW020028271124
451585UK00014B/1511